PROTECTING THE GIRL NEXT DOOR

THE PROTECTORS

SAMANTHA CHASE

NOELLE ADAMS

This book is a work of fiction. Names, characters, places, and incidents are the product of the authors' imaginations or are used fictitiously. Any resemblance to actual events, locales, or persons, living or dead, is coincidental.

Copyright © 2017 by Samantha Chase and Noelle Adams. All rights reserved, including the right to reproduce, distribute, or transmit in any form or by any means.

PROLOGUE
DECLAN

The first time someone called me out on being an asshole with women was when I was eighteen. That someone was my mother.

I was standing in front of the full-length mirror in my bedroom checking myself out in my tux. It was prom, and Amber Collins had insisted I this.

If she was happy with me in the tux, she'd be even happier with me out of it. A slow grin slid across my face as thoughts of how the evening would progress raced through my head.

"Oh, look at you!" my mom said from behind me. "You look so handsome!"

Way to ruin a fantasy.

"Thanks, Mom."

She walked over and smoothed a hand over my jacket and then turned me to face her while she straightened my tie. "Tell me again why the last-minute change in prom dates. I thought you were taking Katie McGrath. The two of you have been talking about it for months.

Yeah. We had, but Katie was... well, Katie was a good girl. A sweet girl. The girl next door that who almost too damn nice. For the three months that we'd dated, I hadn't gotten beyond first base.

First base, for crying out loud.

I was eighteen and in the prime of my life, and Katie was holding on to her virginity card with an iron fist. I just didn't have time for that. I was young and horny and tired of waiting around.

True, there was some statistic about how many teenagers lost their virginity on prom night, but whenever I hinted at it with Katie, she'd become flustered and outraged.

I knew when to cut my losses.

"Declan Curtis," my mother said, snapping me out of my thoughts. "I asked you a question!"

Oh. Right.

"Uh, things just didn't work out. Katie and I weren't right for each other."

"Hmm, you said that about Barbara Kelly too," she murmured.

Ah, Barbara Kelly. Nice enough, great kisser, but she came from a devout Christian home and didn't believe in sex before marriage. And all she talked about was how she couldn't wait to get married and have kids.

I still shuddered at the thought of that conversation.

"And then there was Melanie Baxter," my mom said wistfully. "I really liked her."

That made one of us. We dated for only two weeks, but she was as prim as they came—only let me kiss her on the cheek and hold her hand.

"What can I say, Mom, sometimes things don't work out."

"Oh, stop," she said as she stepped back and looked at me again. "All of those girls were incredibly sweet—so nice and well-mannered. And pretty. I'm telling you, you might not want to admit it, but you seem to have a thing for the fresh-faced girls. You know, the typical girl-next-door type."

Unfortunately, she had a point. There was something to be said for that. All those girls were pretty, but they were just... good. Girls.

And no matter how hard I tried, they never let me make them bad.

After each of those relationships ended—and I always tried to end them on good terms—I always quickly rebounded with some of the naughtier girls. I'd get what I wanted, they'd get what they wanted, and then I'd try it again with another sweet one.

Maybe I had a problem.

The doorbell rang, and my mother looked at me oddly. "I didn't think anyone was coming here. I thought you were picking your date up."

I shrugged. "Nope. Amber hired the limo and said

she'd pick me up. Then we'll head over to pick up some other friends on the way to prom."

"Declan!" she gasped with shock and disbelief. "How could you let that girl come and get you? You should be the one going to get her. It's the only decent thing to do!"

I wasn't really listening. I was already halfway down the stairs.

By the time I pulled the front door open, my mother was behind me, and this time I could have sworn her gasp was followed by a Hail Mary.

I smiled like I had just won the lottery.

Amber Collins was tall and curvy with big breasts that were barely contained behind the tight red satin she was wearing. Her dress was strapless and had a slit that went almost to her hip. Her long blonde hair was loose and curly and her lips matched the dress.

Red and shiny.

I really had won the lottery.

It was going to be a great night.

Behind me, my mother cleared her throat, and I made a quick introduction before posing for a few pictures for her. That seemed to make her happy.

"Okay, Mom, we need to get going."

She gave a serene smile before moving in close. "Declan, may I talk to you for a minute?"

I looked over my shoulder at Amber, who gave the perfect pout at being kept waiting. "We really need to go and pick up the next group."

But she tugged on my arm and led me into the kitchen

and away from Amber. I didn't argue because the sooner she said what she had to say, the sooner I could leave.

"What in the world are you doing with a girl like that?" my mother whispered, smacked my arm.

"Ow! What the... Mom!"

She poked a finger at my chest. "Are you telling me that is the kind of girl you want to go out with?"

"Uh, yeah. That's why I'm going to the prom with her. Are we done here?"

The bland look she gave me told me no.

I sighed. "What is wrong with Amber? You just met her. You have no idea what she's like."

"Oh, I know what she's like," she said, her tone disapproving. "That girl is a wild child if I ever saw one! How could you go from a sweet girl like Katie to *her*?"

"Have you gotten a good look at Amber? She's hot." I said with a grin. "I'm the envy of all the guys at school."

"There is more to a girl than her looks, and shame on you for thinking like that. When you get married, you want it to be to someone with substance. Looks fade, Declan. Remember that."

I seriously rolled my eyes. "Mom, I'm not looking to marry Amber. Hell, I'm not looking to marry anyone. Like ever."

Her eyes went wide even as she gasped again. "You don't know what you're talking about. Of course you'll get married someday."

Now wasn't the time for this conversation.

"Mom—"

"You listen to me, young man," she interrupted. "I am very disappointed that you would give up a relationship with a perfectly sweet girl for someone you just want to show off."

I wanted to do more than just show Amber off, but I wasn't about to tell my mother that.

"Look, I don't expect you to understand. I really don't. But I'm not looking to date the girl next door, fresh-faced, All-American girl. That's who you want me to date. I've tried, and I don't like it. I'm moving on. Amber makes me happy."

"I'm sure she's made many boys happy," she murmured.

Now it was my turn to give her a bland look.

"Don't worry, it's not like this is a serious relationship. I'm not really into that either."

"I swear you're going to be the death of me. I'm going to want grandchildren one day, you know."

That made me laugh.

It was never going to happen.

I didn't ever see myself getting married, and I certainly didn't want kids.

Besides, I was eighteen years old. Why did I even have to think about stuff like this?

Fourteen years later, and I was still cringing at the thought of a wedding. A church, organ music, and flowers. These are not a few of my favorite things.

No matter how hard I try, a wedding reminds me of a funeral. I knew I was here for a wedding, but the tone right now made me think... funeral. Not that I was going to share that thought with anyone—particularly Levi.

I was still kind of shell-shocked by the whole thing. I mean, it didn't seem like that long ago that we were standing in the middle of the desert and just praying we'd come home in one piece. And now? Here we were—four instead of five—standing in the front of a church, wearing tuxedoes and waiting for Harper to walk down the aisle.

Toward Levi.

Toward their future.

I guess it was all good—for them. I still didn't see the point in it. Love, marriage, kids... what was the point anyway? We're here on this earth for a short time. Some shorter than others. Why waste that time trapped in a relationship that most of the time just ends badly?

I looked over at Levi, and he's smiling from ear to ear. Moron. Sure, everything was great right now. They were happy, and they were in love. And they'd just found out that they were going to have a baby. It still blew my mind that it even happened for them. After all, it was a death that brought them together.

And now we're back to funerals.

I shook my head and closed my eyes, trying to force the images from my mind—the desert, the explosion, the funeral. We'd been standing, not much differently than we were right now, waiting to get into position. We were supposed to stay together. We were supposed to have each other's backs, even when we got the signal to move into place. And suddenly it all went wrong.

There were four of us standing at the altar, and there should have been five. I was standing in as the best man, but it just felt wrong. This was Gavin's spot. His place. He would have been Levi's best man—after he kicked Levi's ass for messing with his little sister.

That was the kind of guy Gavin was. He could be pissed off at you one minute, beat the crap out of you, and then buy you a beer. I think we all had a little bit of Gavin in us, but there were times when it hit hard. He wasn't here. And he was never coming back.

I was so lost in my own thoughts that I didn't even realize what was happening until Sebastian elbowed me in the ribs. I looked up and saw that everyone was on their feet and watching Harper walk down the aisle.

I didn't miss the irony. I wasn't paying attention that day in the desert either. Christ. I was seriously losing it. That was probably why the guys were putting me in this new, cushy job. It was idiot work. Glorified babysitting. I didn't understand what Sebastian had meant when he complained about his cushy job—the one where he'd met Ali—but now I did.

At least he had been babysitting adults.

Somehow I got stuck with an actual kid. Me. The guy who avoided anyone under the age of twenty-one. I was the one being thrown to the dogs.

Or the six-year-olds. Same difference.

Somehow I had drawn the short straw and was having to go undercover to protect a kid. Undercover as a teacher. Unbelievable. The kid already had personal security at home, but I had to watch out for her at school in a way that didn't draw unwanted attention.

Right. Like having a guy who basically hates kids and doesn't know what the hell he's doing wasn't going to stick out like a sore thumb.

Suddenly my tie was too tight, and I felt myself breaking out in a sweat. I looked out at the rows of pews. They were filled with people with sappy grins on their faces, sitting there looking at this ceremony as some kind of fairy tale.

I wanted to smack each and every one of them.

Life isn't a fairy tale, and most people don't get their happily-ever-afters. It just doesn't work that way. I mean, I wasn't begrudging or wishing anything bad on Levi and Harper. Hell, I hoped they'd have a good life together. But if they thought it was going to be perfect and all sunshine and unicorns, then they were wrong.

Especially when you threw a baby into the mix.

I had to control myself from rolling my eyes. Kids. Babies. It was like the kiss of death to a relationship. I guess I could have gotten on board with the marriage thing —for other people. Not me. But the whole idea of having babies and kids and doing that whole domestic world... You might as well just hang it all up right then and there because your life would be officially over.

How the hell did I let myself get into this?

I knew that Levi was out of commission for a couple of weeks for his honeymoon, so that left him out of taking my place. Sebastian was knee-deep in an embezzlement case. I glanced over at Cole, who looked as uncomfortable as I felt, and realized that even I couldn't do that to a group of kids. I might not like kids, but I could probably fake it.

Cole would just scare the shit out of them.

So basically, I was screwed.

Another elbow to the ribs reminded me that I had the rings and that I had to get out of my damn head and pay attention to what was going on. Levi looked at me with a stupid grin, and I knew he wasn't mad that I missed my cue, but now I felt like a complete jackass for slacking off. One freaking job to do and I blew it.

Again.

Why did people keep trusting me with important things when clearly I just screwed them up? I already might have cost someone his life. Maybe they thought I'd get better from there. I guess, in comparison, missing my cue for the rings was an improvement. I felt sick to my stomach at even trying to make light of it—even if it was just in my own head.

I was an idiot. I didn't deserve to be up here. Anyone who knew me knew that this was not something I was on board with. The mere fact that Levi asked me to be his best man just showed that he didn't pay attention either.

Gavin.

It should be Gavin.

I was a lousy damn substitute.

How much longer were we going to be up here anyway?

"I now pronounce you husband and wife. You may kiss the bride." The words were barely spoken before Levi had Harper in his arms and was kissing her as if his life depended on it. The preacher stepped back, the organ music swelled, and the whole church stood up and clapped. I joined in. Why not?

Levi and Harper turned and faced their guests, and they were both smiling so damn much that their faces had to hurt. I slapped Levi on the back and congratulated him. He shook my hand and then reached beyond me to shake Seb's hand and then Cole's before turning back to his bride and kissing her again.

I could play the part of the happy groomsman. I could play the part of the guy who believed that people could live happily ever after.

And I guess I was going to have to play the part of the guy who liked being around kids.

Shit.

1

KRISTIN

"Mommy, would you please hurry up?"

The question was posed with impressive gravity and earnestness, despite the fact that it was asked by Lily, my six-year-old daughter.

I piled up the homework handouts I needed to grade tonight and stuffed them into my bag. "You know you have to be patient after school since I can't always leave right away."

Lily gave me a long-suffering frown. "I know. I'm being ex-treme-ly patient."

I tried not to giggle at her conscientious pronunciation of the word.

Lily had long, dark, wavy hair that was presently styled in two very neat braids, and her pink backpack was propped up against her legs. Her hair and blue eyes were like mine, but her seriousness and her smile were just like her dad's.

She wasn't showing me the smile at the moment. I knew it was hard for her to have to hang around after school until I was ready to go. Overall, it was convenient for me to teach fourth grade at the same small, private school my daughter attended—the very same one I attended growing up—but this last half hour as I was scrambling to get things done always dragged for her.

I clasped my bag and then noticed books all over the floor near the bookcase. "Can you run pick those books up for me? I'll just finish erasing the board, and we'll be all done."

She sighed dramatically but didn't argue as she trudged over to the scattered books.

To distract her, I asked, "You had a substitute today, didn't you? How did you like him?"

"Mr. Curtis. He was strange." Lily had squatted down and was busily collecting books.

I paused and glanced over at her. "Strange in what way?"

"He only wanted to play."

I'd only seen the substitute teacher briefly from down the hall. He wasn't on the regular sub list, and I didn't know anything about him. He looked fairly young and had golden-brown hair and an athletic body. Not the typical substitute for a first grade class. "Well, playing can be fun, can't it?"

"I guess, but we didn't do spelling words or math or *anything*." Lily paused from neatly shelving the books and gave me a solemn frown. "I'm going to forget all my subjects before Mrs. Bradbury comes back."

"No, you won't." I made my voice sound cheerful, but I was secretly worried. I'd seen a number of substitute teachers who mostly just filled the day with busy work to make it easy on themselves. If it was just a day or two, then it was no big deal. But Eileen Bradbury was out on maternity leave and wouldn't return for at least ten to twelve weeks.

Lily might just be in first grade, but she couldn't lose that much of her schooling.

"He was probably just getting to know everyone on the first day, and you'll get into your subjects tomorrow."

"I *hope* so."

I slung the strap of my bag over my shoulder and smiled as Lily placed the last books on the shelf. She was very intelligent, and she did everything with infinite seriousness. Sometimes I thought she should have some more fun since she was just six, but reading and schoolwork seemed to be what she found the most fun.

"Ready?" I asked her.

"Yes." She straightened up and pulled on her backpack, which looked almost as big as she was. "I'm ready."

"We can do some reading tonight to make sure you don't forget anything."

She seemed to perk up at this news, and she reached for my hand as we walked down the hall and outside toward the car.

The school was quiet now since students had been

dismissed almost an hour ago. The staff parking lot was about half-empty.

"There he is," Lily announced as I was searching for the keys in my bag. "Mr. Curtis."

I glanced up and over in the direction she indicated and saw a tall man leaning against an SUV across the lot.

He was talking on the phone, and he didn't seem to be aware of our presence.

He really was very good-looking, with broad shoulders, long legs, and that hair that shone a dark gold.

I knew it wasn't right to stereotype, but he didn't look at all like any other substitute first grade teacher I'd ever seen.

He had to be around thirty. If he wanted to be a teacher, then he'd certainly had time to get his certification and get a full-time job by now. I wondered why he hadn't. Maybe he was some kind of a slacker, just hanging around and taking on substitute jobs because they were easy. I hoped that wasn't the case. Not only was that not the kind of teacher I wanted for my daughter—or for any student for that matter—but it also wasn't the kind of teacher we needed for our school. Private schools required a more dedicated type of instructor. And if this man was only looking for an easy paycheck, then...

Okay, I was getting ahead of myself, and Lily had a tendency to easily read my moods. If I continued to stand here scowling, she was going to catch on.

Fast.

"I'm sure things will be better in class tomorrow," I said to Lily, who was frowning in the man's direction.

Like mother, like daughter.

"I hope so." Lily looked up at me with big blue eyes. "I asked him why the sea was salty, and he said I should look it up because right now was playtime."

I hid my immediate indignation at this half-hearted answer to a genuine question from an intelligent girl. "We can look it up when we get home. How about that? I've always wondered why the sea is salty too."

"Okay."

We both climbed into the car, and I glanced once more at Mr. Curtis as I started to pull out of the parking lot. He was still on the phone, and he didn't appear to be having a happy conversation. He was scowling, as if he were angry.

Fight with his girlfriend or something. He was probably really popular with women.

I dismissed the man from my mind as I turned onto the street.

"Do you want to go pick out a Christmas tree this weekend?" I asked, glancing at Lily in the rearview mirror.

I saw her face break into a smile. "Yes! Can we get a really big one?"

"We can get as big a one as will fit in our living room."

"How big is that?"

"I'm not sure. We'll measure it before we go out and look so we'll know exactly how big we can get."

She nodded, obviously thinking deeply on this issue.

I was glad she was excited about the Christmas tree. About Christmas.

Last year had been really hard—being the first Christmas without Nick.

My husband, Nick, had been a SEAL, but he died on a mission a year and a half ago. We'd been married seven years. Sometimes I looked at myself in the mirror and couldn't believe I was a twenty-eight-year-old widow.

But I was. That was me. Living the rest of my life without Nick, who'd been just as sweet and serious as Lily.

We'd grown up together and had been high school sweethearts. It was our love of literature that had first drawn us together in our tenth grade English class. I had known from the first time he read to me from *Pride and Prejudice* that he was the one for me. And just knowing that I'd never hear him do so again was sometimes too much to bear.

As if she'd read my thoughts, Lily said into the silence, "Remember when Daddy brought home the tree that didn't fit."

My throat ached slightly at the memory of Nick cursing under his breath as he tried to get a too-big tree into our small house. "I do remember. He had to chop off the top to make it fit."

Lily giggled. "He wasn't happy."

"But it still looked good, didn't it?"

"Yes. It was pretty. I picked out a bigger star for the top so it didn't look so silly."

"Your daddy always wanted the best for you."

"Yes." She was giving a little nod when I glanced to the mirror to check her expression. "Even the biggest Christmas tree." After a pause, she added, "I remember he liked to read to me."

"He did. He loved books just as much as we do." Nick had loved his job, but he hadn't been what most people thought of in a SEAL. In fact, he'd been thinking of getting out so he could go to graduate school. He'd just about decided on that plan when he'd been killed in action.

If he'd made the decision a little sooner, he might still be alive.

I shook the thought out of my head. Nick had always done his best—in his career, for his family—and there was no use thinking about could-have-beens.

For some reason I pictured again the handsome substitute teacher, leaning against his SUV.

But he was clearly nothing like Nick.

The next morning, I made a point of dropping by Lily's classroom before school started to introduce myself and have a few words with the substitute so I could get a better sense of him.

The kids weren't in the room yet, so I stopped in the open doorway to glance inside. The room was kind of messy, with toys and books not all put up from yesterday. Mr. Curtis was standing in front of the blackboard with a piece of chalk in his hand. He hadn't written anything yet.

He was just staring at the board. I kept waiting for him to write something, but after a few minutes of observing him, I realized he wasn't going to.

Something in the set of his shoulders looked tense, like maybe he didn't want to be here.

I cleared my throat.

He whirled around, obviously surprised, but his face almost immediately relaxed into a smile.

His smile really was amazing—broad and warm and transforming his entire face. Women must just swoon away at the sight of that smile.

Women more vulnerable than me.

"Good morning," I said, feeling strangely awkward for no good reason. I stepped into the room. "I'm Kristin Andrews. I teach fourth grade here, and my daughter Lily is in your class."

He reached to take the hand I extended, his grip warm and strong. He paused a moment before he said, "Oh. Lily. Great. It's nice to meet you. I'm Declan Curtis."

I wondered if he even remembered there was a Lily in his class. His hesitation made me wonder.

It wasn't fair to expect him to know all the kids' names in just one day, but still... I felt a rising of annoyance that I tried to stamp down.

He could be a very nice guy and a perfectly acceptable substitute teacher. No need to jump to conclusions.

"I teach just down the hall. I wanted to introduce myself and see if there was anything you needed." For some reason I thought that sounded stranger than I meant it. "I mean if you had any questions about the school or anything like that."

That sounded better. Right?

"I'm glad you did." He was still smiling at me and still holding my hand, but it felt almost reflexive. As if this was just what he did. Flirt with women as the only way he knew to relate to them.

My annoyance rose even more as I pulled back my hand. "How long have you been teaching?"

"For a while. What about you?"

I was looking for a more specific answer to my question than "a while," but I wasn't sure how to ask it again without sounding outrageously rude. "I've been teaching for eight years. Five years at this school. It's a nice place to work."

"It seems that way." He was still smiling, but I saw that tension again in him. Maybe I was imagining it, but I kept thinking he didn't want to be here.

I tried to relax my smile so it didn't seem forced. "Believe it or not, I used to go to this school. I've lived in the area my entire life. It's a great place for kids and we have a great academic record here that we like to uphold."

He didn't say anything to that, just nodded.

"Anyway, Lily is already a really strong reader. I'm sure you'll discover that soon. Any extra encouragement you can give her would be great since she really wants to keep advancing. She loves school."

"I'll keep that in mind." He hadn't lost that smile. In

fact, it broadened even more. He held my gaze without breaking it.

I suddenly wondered if he was one of those smarmy, charismatic guys who charm their way through life but don't really invest in anything serious. I'd met my fair share of them, and I was starting to recognize the signs.

I took life seriously. So did Lily. We'd both had some really hard things happen to us, but we were getting through them as well as could be expected. It sometimes grated on me that some people could ease through life without taking things seriously.

I tried to stamp down the reaction since it was probably not fair. I'd just known this guy for two minutes, after all.

But I felt like I had a measure of him, and I didn't like it.

"Okay," I said. "Let me know if you need anything. I know it can sometimes be a challenge getting used to a new place."

"Nah," he said, overly casual. "First grade is easy."

I stiffened instinctively. First grade was *not* easy—not if the teacher understood it was important. I was about to go on a bit of a rant about it, but figured that I needed to calm down. It was only his second day here and maybe I was just seeing things that weren't there. "Okay. I'm sure I'll see you around."

I turned around and stepped on a book that shouldn't have been on the floor. It was one of the very thin children's books with slick, paperback covers. There was no traction between it and the floor, and my foot slipped forward slightly.

Maybe I shouldn't have worn these shoes. Teachers at this school could dress fairly casually, but I always tried to dress nice since I was small and looked young, so dressing nice gave me a little extra authority. Even with fourth graders, I'd found it mattered.

Today I wore a straight gray skirt that I thought was flattering without being sexy and a stylish blue top that looked almost vintage and brought out my eyes. My heels weren't super-high, and they were fairly comfortable, but they weren't made for stepping on books that slid on the floor.

I gasped as my whole body jerked with the slide.

I would have caught myself, no trouble, but Declan was there before I knew it, putting an arm around my waist for support.

And, damn it, I liked how it felt. He was big and strong and masculine, and he smelled absolutely delicious—nothing strong or obnoxious, just nice. I leaned against him instinctively for just a minute.

"Are you okay?" he asked, a texture to his voice that made me shiver.

Then I suddenly realized what I was doing, and I straightened up and pulled away quickly. "I'm fine," I murmured. "Thanks. You might want to pick up your classroom."

"Thanks for the advice." He sounded slightly—just slightly—sarcastic.

Frustrated with the entire situation, I walked quickly out of the room without really looking at his face again.

I felt flustered and confused, and I wasn't used to feeling that way. My life since Nick had died had been simple. Straightforward. Revolving around teaching and Lily.

I hadn't had any sort of physical reaction to a man since Nick, which was why it was so upsetting to feel breathless and overly warm right now. When I didn't even like the man.

When I returned to my classroom, I make a conscious effort to brush Declan from my mind.

After all, I certainly wanted there to be the possibility of romance in my life in the future, but if I was going to be attracted to a man again, it would absolutely *not* be to a man like Declan Curtis.

2

DECLAN

"Why, Miss Andrews, I do believe you were checking up on me."

Of course there wasn't anyone here to hear me say it, but there it was. When she first walked in, I was pleasantly surprised. Kristin Andrews was... cute. Totally not my type. That's not to say I don't appreciate a good-looking woman, but I wasn't blown away. She had seemed genuinely sincere when she walked in.

Boy, did that change.

Fast.

I was a fairly good judge of people—I could pick up on body language pretty easily—and that woman was going to be a thorn in my side. I could already feel it. It wasn't only the things that she'd said but the way she'd said them.

Okay, so maybe, just *maybe*, I was a little out of my element here, but it had only been a day. One damn day. Couldn't she cut me some slack? There was no way that any substitute teacher could possibly be expected to get it right after one day. Did she already need to come into my classroom and look down at me?

That thought made me laugh because she was easily five or six inches shorter than me—and that was while she was wearing heels. Sensible heels. I cringed. Yeah, she was going to be making regular appearances here in the classroom to check on me, especially since her daughter... *crap.* What the hell was the kid's name? Lisa? Laura? Lilah? Lily? Yes, Lily. *Whew.*

So now not only did I have my job to do protecting my child client, I also had to be watching over my shoulder for Kristin and her kid. I snorted with disgust. The kid had ratted me out, no doubt. Why couldn't she just be happy? Hell, when I was in school, we used to love the days when there was a substitute. Nonstop playtime and coloring... It was every kid's dream.

Apparently not Lily Andrews's though.

Shit.

The next time I saw Levi, I was going to personally kick him in the throat. There had to be someone else more capable. Or maybe we needed to re-evaluate how we were handling it. This case was so not my thing, and I really didn't have the time or the patience to deal with snooping parents who wanted to pass judgment on me and how I was running this classroom.

Although looking around, it was kind of a mess in here. I hadn't wanted to deal with it yesterday. All I wanted to do was leave by the time the last kid was gone. Who knew a group of six-year olds could be so exhausting? It was too early in the morning for this kind of nonsense. There were books all over the floor, crayons seemingly scattered everywhere, and a ton of shredded paper. Where did all that come from?

I shook my head to clear it and felt my glasses begin to slide. Crap. I had forgotten about them. I thought they made me look a little more studious. They were completely fake—nonprescription and whatnot—but I thought that they might help me in my "role" of teacher.

There were voices out in the hallway, and I knew that my quiet time was up. It was time to get on with the day and figure out how the hell I was supposed to act like I belonged here. My desk was covered in folders and notes from Eileen Bradbury to help me out, but I hadn't even bothered to look at them. It was first freaking grade! Why did I need all this information?

"Hi, Mr. Curtis!"

I looked up and saw one of the kids walk in. I was completely stumped on who it was. I knew she was here yesterday, and she wasn't the kid I was assigned to protect, but her name was a complete blank to me. I could feel myself starting to sweat as the kid put her backpack on her assigned hook and then put her hands on her hips and stared at me with the same judgmental look I had seen only minutes ago.

"Good morning, Lily," I said. I knew that the kid was going to be just as big of a thorn as her mother.

An hour later, I had pretty much gotten the room back in shape. I made a game out of it and let the kids rack up some bonus stars on their behavior chart—whatever the hell that was—and soon everything looked like it had when I arrived yesterday.

Lily's hand was up, and she was practically bouncing in her seat.

"Yes, Lily," I said, trying to sound patient.

"Are we going to work on our math now? Mrs. Bradbury always starts the day with our math assignment."

There were several groans from the other students, and I could tell that no one—other than Lily—was going to be upset if we left the math for later. "Actually, no. Since you guys just did a super job getting the room cleaned up, I figured you'd be a little worn out. Now we're going to... um... we're going to... read. Yeah. Everyone find a book and let's have some reading time. *Quiet* reading time."

"But...," Lily said out loud.

I was about to turn around and go over to my desk, but I did my best to smile sweetly at the kid. "I heard that you enjoy reading," I said, remembering her mother's comments from earlier. "Don't you want to spend some time honing your reading skills?"

"Honing? What's that?" she asked quizzically.

"Uh... I'm sure there's a dictionary in here somewhere. Why don't you look it up?" Geez, why couldn't this kid just be quiet like everyone else. All the other kids had their books out and were reading already.

"But what about math?" she asked.

Now my patience really was wearing thin. I walked over to her desk and crouched down so we were eye level. "Look, Lily," I began, "I'm still going through Mrs. Bradbury's stuff. Things are going to be a little different in here now. I'm the teacher, and we'll do things when I think we need to. Okay?"

She looked up at me with that expression again, and I couldn't believe that I was sitting here explaining myself to a kid. And what was worse, for some reason I still felt like she was winning here somehow.

Levi was so getting his ass kicked.

Standing up, I walked over to my desk and contemplated going through some of the work that Eileen had left for me. But out of the corner of my eye, I saw the newspaper. I hadn't had a chance to read it this morning thanks to Kristin Andrews's inspection.

The kids were all sitting quietly, and for now there was peace in the land. There was a schedule taped to the wall, and I could see that in thirty minutes they had PE and then after that they had art. Awesome! With any luck, I could get through the sports section and then send the kids on their way and have an hour to myself to get my shit together.

I didn't know what I was expecting when I went over the assignment with the guys. I mean, I knew I'd be playing the part of a substitute teacher, but I didn't think I was actually going to be expected to *do* anything—like teaching.

Maybe I would go over the notes while the kids were gone from the classroom, and by the time they got back, I could actually do something that they're expecting. Like math.

I chuckled to myself.

First grade math. How the hell hard could that be?

Mrs. Hilt met fifteen friends. Nine of the friends were carrying pears. The rest were carrying oranges. How many friends were carrying oranges?

My head was still spinning. I must have read that question out loud about a dozen times, and I had no idea how to explain it to the kids. Most of them looked at me blankly, and after finally telling them to use their fingers, I had given up.

Then Lily had pointed out that they couldn't use their fingers because they didn't have fifteen fingers.

The kid was going to be the death of me.

Thank God, I wasn't here to protect her because I might be tempted to turn the other way and let the chips fall where they may.

I was not well. I had to get out of here and figure out how I was going to survive this assignment. School was out for the day—finally—and luckily I didn't have another visit from an inquisitive parent. I scanned the classroom on my way out, and it was a disaster again, but I just couldn't make myself care.

Escape.

I needed to escape and find a way out of this nightmare.

Sprinting across the parking lot, I almost collapsed with relief when I got in my car and closed the door. I was done for the day. No more kids. No more questions. No more math problems.

My phone rang almost immediately, and I was more than ready to give everyone an earful. But I decided to at least wait until Levi was done with his greeting. Barely.

"How's everybody…?"

"I'm gonna kick your fucking ass, man," I snapped, effectively cutting him off. "I can't *believe* that you put me on this case!"

"Okay, I believe Declan has the floor," Levi said wearily. "Is everyone here?"

Sebastian and Cole both chuckled their response, and I wanted to reach through the phone and strangle them. I couldn't believe that they had the balls to laugh right now. "Do you have any idea what the hell I'm dealing with here?"

"Not really," Levi said. "But I'm sure you're about to tell us. So why don't you just get on with it."

Where did I even begin? "Are any of you aware of what the average first grader has to learn these days?" I didn't wait for any answers. "It's insane! The list of stuff that I'm expected to go through with them is fucking crazy! And on top of that, I just got handed some sort of sign-up sheet for a Christmas pageant! A Christmas pageant! I don't even know what the hell that is, but apparently all the teachers are expected to contribute something that they prepare with their class!"

"You mean like a picture?" Cole asked, barely containing his mirth.

"No, douchebag, I'm talking like a song or something." I was so fucking screwed that I couldn't even stand it. "I don't understand all the instructions that this teacher left for me. The kids don't understand anything that I say. The classroom is a mess, and I've got parents starting to breathe down my neck."

I was practically out of breath by the time I'd spit all that out. "You've got to get someone else to do this, Levi. I'm serious. This is so not my thing."

"Yeah, yeah, I get that," Levi said. "Let's put playing teacher aside for a minute and talk to me about our clients. Have you met with them?"

I sighed. Loudly. "I met with them over the weekend. Jackson Vanderhall, age forty-five. He and his trophy wife are currently in a custody battle over their daughter. Their divorce isn't final yet because of the custody issue."

"What's holding it up?" Cole asked. "I mean, I know this is a custody case, but I don't see how this involves us."

"Mrs. Vanderhall—also known as Mitzi—was a teenage beauty queen. Jackson married her when she was nineteen, and she was pregnant at twenty. Since their daughter's birth, Mitzi has been obsessive about the kid following in her footsteps."

"I'm still not seeing…"

"The kid doesn't want to do it, Jackson doesn't want her doing it, but the mom hasn't listened. She puts the kid in pageants whenever and wherever she can without Jackson's consent."

"Hey, maybe they can help you with the Christmas pageant," Sebastian joked.

"Fuck you," I growled. "Anyway, there's more." I really hated this shit. "There have been allegations of abuse."

"By which spouse?" Cole asked.

"Jackson is saying that his wife has become physically abusive to the kid when she complains about being in the pageants. Right now there was enough physical evidence to get a judge to rule on supervised visitations, but Jackson's afraid that Mitzi's going to try to steal the kid. That's why I'm here at the school. I have to keep an eye on her and make sure that no one comes near her except her father."

"Why only at school? Why aren't we doing this full time?" Sebastian asked.

"They have someone at home and have security in place. They needed someone here to blend in and not raise any suspicion."

"Right," Cole said dryly. "Because you blend."

"Okay, enough," Levi said. "So have you seen anything at school yet? Anything that looks amiss?"

"No. Actually, the kid hasn't been in the past two days.

Jackson took her to Disney for a week, and she'll be back tomorrow. I was supposed to use these days to get used to the whole classroom thing."

"Which you're not having any luck with," Cole said.

"You think?" I said sarcastically and then tried to relax. "I am so out of my comfort zone here, guys. I... I really don't think I can do this. There's like twenty-four kids in the class, and I'm expected to remember their names. It took me a year to remember your names, and there's only three of you!"

"You're panicking, that's all," Levi said calmly. "It will get easier. You need to just try to calm down. Have you remembered any of their names?"

"Well... yeah. There's... Kenny. He eats paste. And Monica. She wears the most obnoxious hair bows."

"When did hair bows get obnoxious?" Cole laughed.

"You're really starting to piss me off," I snarled. "And then there's the kid I'm here for."

Levi chuckled.

"What? What's so funny?" I asked through clenched teeth.

"Say it. Say her name," Levi said, and I knew that he was probably biting his own fist to keep from laughing. "Come on. Prove to us that you have her name memorized."

Shit. "Jessileigh," I muttered.

"I'm sorry," Sebastian said, humor lacing his voice. "What was that?"

"I said her name is... Jessileigh."

"What the hell kind of name is that?" Cole asked.

"A beauty-queen-in-training name," I said.

"Okay, so you've got... three whole names memorized. Good for you."

"Don't patronize me, Levi," I said. "And then there's Lily."

"Who's she?" Sebastian asked.

"She's in my class, and her mom is a teacher here. The kid ratted me out, I think, because her mom came in and introduced herself this morning."

"So because a fellow teacher introduced herself, you think that the kid ratted you out? Paranoid much?" Cole asked.

"Oh, she didn't come in to introduce herself so much as she came in to... inspect and pass judgment."

"Yeah, okay," Levi said. "There's no time to deal with your insecurities, Dec. You've got a job to do, and you need to quit whining about it. This case is important—a child's welfare is at stake. You need to suck it up and do what you're there to do."

"It's not so cut and dried, you know! I'm not just looking after the kid..."

"Jessileigh," he corrected.

"Fine. Jessileigh. I'm expected to teach a room full of kids! What the hell do I know about teaching the first grade?"

"You obviously passed the first grade," Sebastian said. "How hard can it be?"

"Maybe I need to go and talk to the principal and see what the bare minimum is that I can get away with."

"No," Levi said, more firmly this time. "You are going to shut up and man up and follow the damn rules and do your job. Are we clear?"

It wasn't like Levi to be so... boss-like. Unfortunately, he had a point. I'd never had a challenge that I couldn't handle. I'd never shied away from any task. I was the confident one, the cocky one, the one that made fun of other people's insecurities.

It was time to put on my big-boy pants and get to work.

And brush up on my first grade math.

I was feeling pretty confident the next morning. I spent the entire night going over the notes Eileen had left for me and basically learning the essentials of the first grade.

Not a good feeling for a guy who had passed the first grade almost twenty-five years ago.

So there I was, walking down the hall, a little spring in my step, when I looked up and saw... her. Kristin was heading my way, and part of me wanted to do a quick sidestep into the nearest open doorway. Avoidance wasn't usually my thing, but if Lily complained to her mother again... Well, I didn't need Kristin bringing me down. Not when I was feeling good about what I'd accomplished.

"Mr. Curtis," she said with a sincere smile as she approached.

That instantly made me suspicious, but I forced myself to remain calm. "Ms. Andrews. How are you today?" I hated polite, social chitchat.

"Fine. Thanks." She eyed the stack of books and folders in my arms, and her smile seemed to grow. "It looks like you had a lot of homework last night."

"You could say that," I said evenly. We stood there in amicable silence for a minute, and that was when it hit me. Kristin Andrews wasn't "cute"—not like I had thought yesterday. Looking at her now—with a little more of a relaxed attitude—I noticed that she was really quite attractive. She had a girl-next-door thing going on that was kind of appealing.

I had to force myself to look away because suddenly I found myself having some inappropriate thoughts swirling in my head about *this* particular girl next door.

"I hope the kids aren't giving you too hard of a time. They tend to take advantage when there's a substitute in the room."

There was no condescension in her tone, and that made me relax even more. Maybe we had just gotten off on the wrong foot yesterday. She had a really great smile, and I felt myself being suddenly drawn to her. "I'll admit that they're a little tougher than I'd expected." We both chuckled at that, and Kristin rested her hand on my arm.

And that one innocent gesture felt more intimate than anything I'd felt in a long time.

"Never underestimate a six-year-old. They can be bossy and opinionated and..." She sighed. "Great."

"You've got a great daughter," I heard myself say.

Kristin nodded. "Yes, I do." Her eyes met mine, and it was all I could do to stop myself from leaning in and resting my forehead on hers right before I kissed her.

Wait. Kiss her? What?

This woman was a co-worker, a parent to one of my students, and that meant she was most likely married too. I had to get my head on straight and stop looking and thinking about her in any capacity that wasn't strictly professional.

Off in the distance, I could hear people starting to walk around the hallway. I cleared my throat and took a step back. What the hell was I thinking? I was here to do a job. I had a kid to protect and a group of kids who were expecting me to be teaching them… something. Anything.

I looked at Kristin and saw the same dazed expression on her face I was sure was on mine.

Glad to see I wasn't alone.

"I… I better go," she said, suddenly seeming shy. "I hope you have a good day."

I cleared my throat again and took another small step away. "Um…yeah. You too. Thanks."

And without another word, she walked away.

And damn if I didn't stand there and watch the soft sway of her hips as she made her way down the hall.

3

KRISTIN

Rose Dwyer had been the school secretary for as long as I'd been teaching here. She was an attractive woman in her thirties who was single and perpetually looking for a man.

I'd always liked her, and she was invariably my source if I needed news on anything going on at the school.

A week later, when I'd stopped by the office to check my box, I paused by her desk to chat and find out a little more about Declan Curtis, whose teaching I was getting increasingly worried about.

"So what's the word on the guy who's subbing in first grade?" I asked after I'd inquired about her weekend and heard about her date from hell.

She gave an exaggerated sigh and raised her hand to her chest. "Isn't he dreamy? Every unmarried woman in the school is asking me about him, so you're going to have some competition. I just love a sexy guy in glasses."

I was so surprised by the comment that I gaped for a few seconds. "*What*? I'm not interested in him."

"Well, why not? He's gorgeous and charming and obviously likes kids. What more could you want?"

I shouldn't have been shocked at the swooning look in Rose's eyes since the man was obviously daydream material—if you only cared about superficial qualities. But I definitely didn't want anyone thinking I was interested in him. I could just imagine how the gossip around the school would spin out of control if that idea got started. "I'm sure he's great, but he's not my type."

I thought about my reactions to our brief encounters and had to remind myself very strongly that he was absolutely *not my type*.

"I guess not." Rose's smile shifted slightly. "I guess your type is tall, dark, and serious. Like Nick."

"Yeah. Nick was my type." I felt a familiar pang at the thought of my dead husband, but the grief no longer crippled me the way it had during the first year after he'd died. "Anyway, I wanted to know what the word is on this guy in terms of his teaching. Where did he teach before? Why is he just subbing instead of getting a regular teaching job?"

"I'm not sure," Rose admitted. "I figured maybe he's got some sort of personal issue going on. Or maybe he's new to the area and a temp position is the only thing he could find right now. I wouldn't be surprised if he's hoping this will turn into a full-time job though."

"How much experience did he have before?"

"I don't know."

"Didn't you look at his application?"

"No. Chuck took care of all that himself."

Chuck was the principal of the school, and he usually let Rose handle the application process for new teachers—so this surprised me. Why didn't anyone know about this guy's background? "So you don't know where he taught before?"

"I don't. But he must have a good background, or Chuck wouldn't have given him the job over our regular subs. There haven't been any complaints or anything from students or parents, and Chuck goes to stop by the class to observe a few times a day."

"He looks in on the class that often? If he doesn't think the guy knows what he's doing, then why give him the position at all?"

Rose gave a little shrug. "I don't know. But I'm not complaining. Nothing like a little eye candy to make the day a little brighter."

I managed not to sneer since I really did like Rose most of the time, and I didn't want her to see how annoyed I was that she was swooning over Declan Curtis.

After all, it wasn't like he was so drop-dead gorgeous that a sensible woman would turn into an idiot. He was attractive enough, with those golden looks of his, but I hadn't seen anything else to impress me.

"Do you not like him for some reason?" Rose asked, evidently catching something in my expression.

"I don't know him. I've only seen him around. But Lily says that he's not really teaching them anything." I paused. "Let's just say that so far I'm not overly impressed."

"It's first grade."

"I know it's first grade, but that doesn't mean the day needs to be wasted on frivolous activities. There's a lot kids need to learn during that year, and it's not right if this guy isn't taking it seriously."

"I'm sure he is. He's just probably one of those teachers who can turn learning into such fun that kids hardly notice they're learning."

"Lily knows if she's learning or not." I let out a breath, telling myself to be patient and not jump to unfair conclusions. Maybe he was easing into things and he'd start buckling down soon.

He'd had more than a week now though, and nothing had changed in the classroom, according to Lily.

"Maybe she's learning things and doesn't realize it."

"Or maybe he's just treating teaching like a game. Like it's not really important work. Teaching isn't easy. Not just anyone can do it."

"I know that." Rose smiled in a particular way. "You're really riled up. I don't think I've ever seen you this riled up before."

"Yes, I'm riled up. Teaching is important. First grade is important. And it shouldn't be thrown away on an overgrown kid, no matter how sexy he is."

The momentum of my words had caused me to step back and raise my voice slightly. Then I noticed Rose's expression change, and her eyes shifted to something over my shoulder.

I froze, realizing immediately what her distraction meant. Someone else was in the office.

When I turned to look, I saw Declan leaning against the doorframe with his typical leisurely confidence. He had a half smile on his face.

I was momentarily overwhelmed with mortification, wondering how much he'd heard and if it was obvious I was talking about him.

I didn't like the man, but I never would have laid him out right to his face.

Then he gave me a little wink, evidently not caring at all about what he'd just overheard.

I sucked in an indignant breath and turned away. The man was absolutely infuriating. Didn't he take anything seriously at all?

To keep myself from saying something unforgivably rude, I turned away and walked over to the shelf of staff mailboxes. The handouts for today's classes I'd needed copied were in there, so I grabbed them, taking a minute to pull myself together again.

"You're looking particularly ravishing today, Rose," I heard Declan saying behind me in a tone that was light, almost playful.

I tried not to roll my eyes. It was probably habitual with him. He was the type to flirt with anyone of the female variety.

Rose giggled in response.

I smoothed down my skirt with one hand as I turned around. Today I was wearing one of what Lily called my "teacher dresses"—a belted blue shirtdress that was comfortable and looked slightly old-fashioned. It was flattering enough but definitely didn't look "ravishing."

And for some reason, that bothered me.

"Have a good day, Rose," I said with a smile. Then I nodded to Declan out of general civility.

He grinned at me as he walked over to check his mailbox too.

I was glad to be rid of him as I left the office, so I was surprised and not at all pleased when I realized he'd followed me and had fallen in step with me as I walked down the hall toward my classroom.

He was probably going to his classroom too.

I wished—I really, really wished—I didn't feel a rush of attraction as I looked up at his handsome face and warm grin.

"So how is your class going?" I asked, trying to sound natural and not like he'd flustered me.

He had, but he didn't need to know it.

"You tell me." His expression was slightly smug, as if he knew I had doubts about him.

"Lily says you give the students a lot of free time."

"It's good for them. They enjoy it."

"Yes, but they're just in first grade, and they need structure to learn."

He paused in front of his classroom and looked down

at me like he could see a lot deeper into my head than he should. "I bet you need structure too."

"What does that mean?"

He gave an amused shrug. "You look like the kind of woman who likes structure. Everything neat and orderly and according to plan. When was the last time you did something spontaneous?"

"I don't have time or energy for much spontaneity. I have a class full of fourth graders and Lily to raise."

"I'm sure her dad must help a little."

I felt my spine stiffen. Declan obviously didn't know about my marital situation. He still had that almost lazy, flirtatious look about him—as if he were used to charming the pants off women without even trying. He wasn't coming on to me or anything. It was likely just his habitual manner. "Lily's dad is dead," I said, making sure my voice was mild so I didn't sound upset or angry with him for bringing it up.

His expression instantly changed. "Sorry."

"Don't be. You didn't know. But he liked structure too, as a matter of a fact. He was a SEAL."

He glanced away from my face briefly before he looked back. "I was a Marine. I know what it's like to lose someone."

He wasn't looking particularly intense or deep or serious, but I could tell he meant it. He had lost someone he cared about. He did know how it felt. He understood.

And the attraction I'd been feeling for him heightened

so quickly it left me breathless. For the first time, I felt like he was more than a good-looking waste of space.

Suddenly there was a connection, a bond, and I had no idea how I felt about it.

I cleared my throat, telling myself I needed to get it together quick. It was fine if I was starting to think about men again—I wasn't going to feel guilty about that—but I was all screwed up if I was thinking in the direction of Declan.

He just wasn't the kind of man it was smart to take seriously.

"How long were you in the Marines?" I asked, genuinely curious since I still wanted to put his background together.

He opened his mouth to respond automatically but then closed it again. Then said, "A few years."

"Where did you go to college?"

"Why do you want to know?" He stepped closer to me, so much so that he was definitely in my personal space.

I lost my breath again, since his body was so close, so big, so masculine. I suddenly wanted to touch it. "Just curious. It's a normal question, isn't it?"

"I don't know."

"Well, you said you were a Marine, so I just wondered how college and teaching fit into that. Did you go to college first and then join the Marines? Or did you go back to school after you got out?"

"Why don't we have coffee some time, and you can ask

me all about my background." There was a particular drawl to his tone that was impossible not to recognize.

Was he actually asking me out? He wouldn't even answer the most simple of questions about his background, and yet he thought I was so easy that I'd still fall under his spell. "I don't think so," I said, making sure my voice was almost gentle, rather than biting off his head the way I really wanted. "You're my daughter's teacher. And on top of that, I don't have a lot of free time for things like going out for coffee." I paused and let that sink in before adding, "I need to get to my class."

I walked down the hall toward my classroom, soon feeling calm again and more myself.

It wasn't like he was the first guy to ever ask me out, even after Nick had died. I'd lived a very quiet life for the past two years, but I shouldn't let something as little as this fluster me so much.

As I opened the door to my classroom, I realized that Declan hadn't answered a single one of my questions. And I suddenly wondered if he'd asked me out just to get me to leave him alone.

"I did good on my story, Mommy," Lily said that afternoon as she was emptying her backpack as she always did after we got home from school.

"You did *well*," I corrected automatically.

"I did well," she repeated, not troubled at all by the correction. She always liked to learn.

"Did you?" I was slicing up an apple for her, but I glanced over my shoulder to see the piece of paper she was holding. "I'd like to read it."

"Okay. Do you want me to read it to you?"

"That would be great."

As I finished getting her afternoon snack together, she read out in a slow, precise voice. "*I like trees. I like to climb trees. I have a tree in my yard that I climb. I sit on a branch and have fun. I never fall.*"

"That's really good, Lily." I brought the sliced apple and cheese over to the kitchen counter, where she was sitting on her stool. "You used some hard words in that."

"I know. Mr. Curtis said it was perfect and gave me a star."

"That was great." I was feeling better—and slightly guilty—since obviously they'd been practicing some real writing in class. I scanned the piece of paper on which she'd written her sentences and drawn a brown-haired girl in a tree. "Oops, you spelled 'climb' wrong. There's a *b* at the end of it."

Lily frowned soberly down at her paper. "There is?" She reached over and grabbed a pen from the cup we kept them in and carefully wrote a *b* at the end of the word. "Like this?"

"Right. Perfect."

"Why is there a *b* at the end? We don't say clim-b."

"No, but it's a silent *b*. Sometimes it's there and you can't hear it."

"Why didn't Mr. Curtis tell me I got it wrong?" She was breathing heavily, obviously upset about her mistake. She'd always been a little perfectionist.

"You did really well with it. He was probably glad you did so well."

"But he said I did perfect."

I was kind of upset too—not that Lily had misspelled a word but that he hadn't corrected her. How was she supposed to learn unless he told her? I had to wonder again if it was just a kind of smug laziness—thinking first grade was easy, that it didn't matter. Or that no one would notice.

Maybe he didn't even notice.

"He probably meant you did really well. And you drew a beautiful tree. I really like how you did the bark."

"I tried to make it look scratchy like bark is, so I did the triangles."

I stroked her dark hair as she studied her picture, looking pleased again. "You did an amazing job. I never would have thought to draw bark that way."

That evening, I was still thinking about Declan Curtis and his unwillingness to answer any questions about his background.

Something strange was going on here.

I knew if Chuck was looking in on him regularly, that the kids weren't likely to be in any danger from him, but I didn't want Lily to go three months without a teacher who actually wanted her to learn.

So after she went to bed for the night, I did a web search on his name.

There were quite a few hits about his time in the Marines, including a number of articles about an accident that had killed another soldier when he'd been present. At least he'd been honest about knowing what it was like to lose someone, if it had been a friend of his who'd died. He must have just gotten out a year or so ago, which meant he must have gone to college before he'd joined up.

I searched through the results but couldn't find anything referencing a college. I saw a couple of brief references to a security firm, but that must be a different Declan Curtis.

He'd evidently been born in Fairfax, Virginia. And I found one of those look-up-your-old-classmates sites that listed him as having gone to high school there. But no college was listed.

I supposed not everyone's college could be found through an online search, but something was strange here. I had the dates of his high school years, which put him at around thirty-two years old. I had references to his being in the Marines going back for several years. Assuming he was in college for four years, that didn't leave any time to get teaching experience.

What the hell was he doing subbing in our little private school?

My first thought was to go to Chuck with my concerns, but that felt rather underhanded.

I preferred to be honest and straightforward whenever I could, so I'd go talk to Declan tomorrow morning and see if I could get answers to my questions.

If he blew me off again, then I'd go to Chuck.

He sure as hell better not try to distract me by asking me out again. What kind of a pushover did he think I was, to be diverted from genuine questions by a pair of broad shoulders and a sexy grin?

A very sexy grin.

I really wished I hadn't started thinking about that, just as I was getting ready for bed.

The next morning, I stopped by his classroom first thing before the kids arrived.

He was crouching down in front of the little bookcase, shelving books quickly and rather haphazardly.

I swallowed at the site of his fine, tight butt in his khakis but made myself push the thought from my mind. I cleared my throat.

It evidently startled him because he jumped to his feet in an automatic posture of defense.

Nick used to do the same thing when he was startled. Too many years of being in harm's way.

"Sorry to surprise you," I said mildly.

"It's fine." His posture and face relaxed until it had that flirtatious half smile again. "And how are you this morning?"

I suddenly hated that look. It was like he hid behind it or something. "I'm fine. I was thinking about our conversation yesterday..."

"Yeah?" he prompted, sounding a bit hopeful. He was probably thinking that I had reconsidered his offer to go for coffee.

"I wanted to ask you again about where you went to college."

He blinked. "What?"

"Where did you go to college? And when? And what is your previous experience teaching? I did a little research, and the dates I found don't seem to add up, so I wanted to ask you about it."

He came over to where I stood, his presence shifting until it felt almost intimidating. "Why does it concern you?"

My mouth fell open briefly. "Because I'm a teacher at this school, and my daughter is a student in your class. I think I'm entitled to know your background so I can be confident that these kids are in good hands."

"You have nothing to worry about."

"Well, please excuse me if I don't feel comfortable taking you at your word. I don't know you. And my daughter is in your class. If you'll tell me about your education and previous experience, then I won't have to keep pestering you about it."

His eyes narrowed, and I realized he was bristling—like *I* was the one being inappropriate or unreasonable here. "And if I don't?"

"Then I'll have to talk to Chuck. I'm sorry. I promise I'm not in the habit of causing people trouble just because, but this is too important for me to ignore. I can't think of any reason you won't tell me the answers to simple questions, unless you have something to hide."

"It's not really your business what I'm hiding." His voice had grown gruffer, and there was something really sexy about his looming intensity—much more attractive than his characteristic manner.

My body was definitely interested in this man. No doubt about that.

But I didn't have to let my body decide my behavior. This was too important.

"Of course it's my business. Should I not care about my daughter's welfare?"

"Your daughter is perfectly safe with me."

"I also want her to learn, you know."

"She already knows twice as much as the rest of the class. And I'll tell you this." For just a moment he looked almost fierce. "I don't respond well to threats."

I raised myself up to my full height, which just wasn't very high. "And I don't respond well to people trying to hide things that I have a right to know."

I could tell by his expression that nothing constructive

was going to come out of this conversation. He wasn't going to tell me anything I wanted to know.

I hated the thought of tattling to the principal, but what else could I do?

I'd seen too often the serious, negative consequences of letting suspicious things go when it came to kids.

I wasn't going to let this go.

4

DECLAN

HOUSTON, WE HAVE A PROBLEM.

I'd been around my share of difficult women before, but seriously? This one took the cake. I got that this was a private school, and I would even concede that she had the right to be curious, considering her daughter was in the class. But what Kristin Andrews was doing right now bordered on harassment. What was she, some sort of fucking narc?

Like this assignment wasn't shitty enough, now I had to watch my back against some uptight woman who clearly had some control issues.

Shit.

Well, two could play at this game. If she wanted to make some waves, then just let her try. She'd be fighting a losing battle because, right now, I was going to beat her to the punch. I looked up and saw that there was still time before the students started to arrive and stalked down to the main office.

"Hey, Rose," I said smoothly, flashing her a grin. "Has Chuck come in yet?"

"He just arrived a few minutes ago. You'll find him back in his office." She gave me a smile of her own, and as stupid as it sounded, it restored my faith in the female of the species. At least *some* people weren't suspicious of me.

I knocked on Chuck's door with a little more force than was necessary, and he jumped at the sound. "Sorry. Can I talk to you for a minute?"

"Absolutely," he said and gestured for me to take a seat. "How are things going? Did you get through the papers last night with the system we talked about?"

Yesterday, Chuck and I had our daily, after-school meeting, and he gave me some advice on how to get through grading homework without wanting to stab my own eyes out. It wasn't much help, but I didn't need a shot of whiskey either to get through it.

"It went fine. Thanks." I shifted in my seat and tried to think of the best way to approach this issue.

"What's on your mind, Declan? Is it the class? Is it Jessileigh? Has there been any news there?"

"No, no. Nothing like that. So far everything has been quiet on that front." I took a deep breath and decided to just spit it out. "There's a problem with a parent. Actually, she's more than a parent... She's a... She's one..." *Shit.* "She's a teacher here. Kristin Andrews. Her daughter is in my class, and she's been asking all kinds of questions about my qualifications and about how I run the class and... Dammit, Chuck, she's all but threatening me at this point. What is her deal?"

"Kristin? Threatening you?" Chuck let out a laugh. "I'm sorry, but that's so out of character for her. She's normally a very agreeable person. The students and faculty love her. She gets along with everybody."

"Obviously not," I said, and I was beginning to feel a little less confident than I had ten minutes ago.

Shaking his head, Chuck sat down behind his desk. "Kristin's one of our alumni. She's lived in this town her entire life and I've never heard of her having an issue with anyone. Heck, I've never even heard her say anything negative about anyone. Honestly, Declan, she's a sweetheart. Are you sure you're not just over-thinking this? Maybe you're just stressed because of how overwhelmed you've been feeling and you're taking what she's saying the wrong way."

"Trust me, I'm not taking anything the wrong way," I said through clenched teeth.

For a minute, Chuck just sat there in confusion and then started spouting out more praise for Kristin—great student, great teacher, involved in the community, blah, blah, blah.

Leave it to me to be the one person who didn't think of Kristin Andrews as America's sweetheart.

"Look, we didn't discuss giving me a background because it shouldn't have come up. All the other parents have been great. But I have to be honest with you, I can't do battle with this woman every damn day. She can clearly tell that I'm not a teacher, and I can't tell her what's going on and risk Jessileigh's safety."

Chuck instantly sobered. "No, you're right." He huffed out a slightly frustrated breath. "What are her complaints exactly?"

Where did I even begin? "Her daughter is the smartest kid in the class. I haven't ever taught before or been around kids, but I can see that she's way beyond a first grade level in everything. Basically, Lily is complaining that we're not doing enough."

"You don't hear of that happening very often—a student complaining about not enough work."

"Tell me about it," I mumbled. "I'm doing the best I can in regards to the teaching, Chuck. You and I discussed this. I never claimed to be a teacher. My main concern is Jessileigh and keeping her safe. I am careful to almost never let that little girl out of my sight while she's here at school. Kristin Andrews is a problem, and I need you to get her to back off."

"It's not that easy, Declan. She's a teacher here as well as a parent. It's not like I can ask her to not talk to you."

"Throw me a bone here, Chuck. I have a job to do, and I can't have some nosy parent distracting me. Can't you talk to her? Feed her some bullshit to shut her up. Make up a college that I went to, tell her that you have fourteen golden references to my character and teaching ability... I don't care. Just... get her to back off."

My frustration was coming through loud and clear, and

I wasn't proud of it. I'm a fucking Marine, dammit. I should be able to handle one tiny woman—no matter how annoying she was! I hated that this was what I was reduced to. A first grade teacher running to the principal because someone was trying to bully me.

There was no way I was sharing this with the guys.

No way in hell.

"I'll have a conversation with her today or tomorrow, Declan. You have my word." He stood and held out a hand, and I shook it.

"Thanks, Chuck. I appreciate it."

I walked out of his office and through the reception area and winked at Rose. She blushed. She was cute enough but not someone that I was really interested in.

Damn. As soon as that thought entered my brain, the only face that came to mind as someone I was interested in was the girl next door.

Kristin Andrews.

"I just can't catch a fucking break, can I?"

"Okay, Jess..."

"It's Jessileigh," the little girl said quietly. "My mom says that Jess is a boy's name."

Right now I'd love to get my hands on Mrs. Mitzi Vanderhall and shake her. I'd been sitting with Jessileigh since the class got back from lunch. Everyone was working in groups to identify different plants. There was a nice garden set up outside the first grade classrooms—all two of them—and the other teacher had agreed to take my kids out with hers while I worked with Jessileigh.

"So what's the problem?" I asked carefully. When I went to line the class up to go outside, Jessileigh had stayed at her desk and refused to budge. Luckily, Robin Moore—the other first grade teacher—had come to my rescue. "Why don't you want to go out in the garden?"

She looked at her hands, which were folded in her lap, and even I could tell that she was nervous. The poor kid never looked like she was comfortable. From her first day back in class, I was able to see that the kid was obviously feeling the pressure of her parents' situation.

"I... I... I'm not supposed to get dirty. This is a new dress and... if I get anything on it... I'll be in trouble."

Ah. Okay. Now we were getting somewhere. "How about if I promise that you won't get anything on your dress?"

She looked up at me with the biggest blue eyes I had ever seen. They were so big and so sad that something tugged at my heart. I could tell that she wanted to say something but wasn't sure of herself.

"What if I assigned you a buddy?"

"A buddy?"

I nodded. "Someone that would work with you and only you so you won't be in a group and you could go at your own pace. How would you like that?"

Without a word, she simply nodded.

And then smiled shyly.

"Okay." Standing, I went to the back door of the classroom that opened up to the garden. I looked out at the group and knew that they still had a good thirty minutes of exploring time, and I wanted to make sure that Jessileigh had the opportunity to participate. I wracked my brain for a minute, trying to remember if there was anyone in the class that Jessileigh was friends with. Unfortunately, I knew for a fact that the little girl spent most of her time by herself.

"Lily?" I called out. "Can you come here, please?"

This could quite possibly kill two birds with one stone. First Lily could help Jessileigh with the assignment in a nonintimidating way, and second, it would give Lily more responsibility and therefore make her feel like she was doing more.

And get her mother off my back.

"Yes, Mr. Curtis?" she asked as she skipped over to the door.

"I have a very important job for you," I began, hoping to pique her interest.

"You do?" Her eyes went wide, and I almost grinned.

"How would you like to be a helper?" I have to admit, the idea literally just came to me. Jessileigh needed someone to help her, and I needed something that was going to make Lily Andrews focus on something other than my shortcomings.

"A helper?" she asked, carefully considering my words. "What's that?"

I crouched down and carefully explained to her about

Jessileigh's concerns about walking around in the garden. "I thought that you would make an excellent helper. You could show her all the different plants and flowers and, you know, make sure that she doesn't have any problems."

For a minute I thought the kid was going to turn me down. She looked up at me with that same look that her mother usually gave me while she considered her options.

"I didn't want to ask just anyone to do this, Lily," I said, doing my best to convince her. "I know you're the number one science student and you'll know exactly how to show Jessileigh the right stuff without making her get too hands-on. So what do you say? Will you be a helper?"

She studied me for another minute. "Will I get an extra star on my science chart?"

I almost wanted to kiss her. "Sweetheart, if you help Jessileigh out with this assignment, I'll give you two extra stars."

I saw her eyes go wide again right before she high-fived herself. "Deal."

Without another glance in my direction, I watched her walk across the classroom and over to Jessileigh. Two minutes later, the two of them walked outside like they were the best of friends.

Maybe I didn't totally suck at this teacher thing.

I was relieved when I looked up and saw that the end-of-the-day bell was about to ring. I lined the kids up and prepared to dismiss them and made sure that Jessileigh was at the back of the line.

Our general routine was that all the bus riders got dismissed first, then the carpool group. Jessileigh fell into the second group, but I always walked her out and waited with her until her father's car pulled up.

The bell rang, and the first group walked out—following one of the assistant teachers who handled the task on a rotating basis. Three minutes later, the second bell rang for the carpool group. Jessileigh and I followed at the back of the group like we always did. I felt more secure knowing that no one was behind us.

Usually we made the walk in silence, but today the kid seemed to have a lot to say.

"Lily showed me the daisies and the sunflowers. Yellow is my favorite color, and both of those flowers had yellow in them. I think I'm going to draw of picture of them as part of our science homework. Would that be okay, Mr. Curtis?"

I was stunned silent by the amount of words the kid just spewed out at me. Looking down at her, I noticed that a bit of the sadness that usually clouded her eyes was gone. It made me smile.

"Sure. I think that would be a great idea." We made it to the front door, and we stayed back and watched as the line of cars flowed through. I had to hand it to the kid. She was a trooper. She never complained and did what she was told. I knew that the situation with her parents was a bad one and it was taking its toll on her, but she held it together.

"Do you... do you think that Lily could be my buddy in art class tomorrow?" she asked shyly.

Her eyes didn't meet mine, but I crouched down and looked at her until she did. "I think that's a great idea. I'm sure she'd really enjoy that."

I stood up and looked out the door and saw the black BMW pull up to the curb. "Your dad's here," I said, and together we walked out to the car. I waited until she was safely inside and buckled up before stepping back and watching them drive away.

As much as I wanted to talk to Jackson Vanderhall, we had agreed that all communications would be done over the phone so that we didn't upset Jessileigh and didn't draw attention to ourselves on school property. I made a mental note to call him later and let him know that his daughter was finally starting to feel comfortable enough with me to start opening up about some of her fears.

Progress.

Walking back to the classroom, I knew I had about twenty minutes worth of cleanup to do before I could leave with a clear conscience. There was a ton of handouts to grade—all of which I planned on doing at home—and I was just ready to have some time to myself with no chattering six-year-olds surrounding me.

Picking up books was its own brand of torture and something that seemed to be never ending. I was in the middle of clearing up the reading corner when I heard someone enter the room. I turned and forced myself to smile.

Lily.

"Hey, Lily. Did you forget something?"

She shook her head and slowly walked over to me. The kid was totally transparent. There was something on her mind, and she was trying to gather up the courage to talk to me.

Stopping about three feet away, Lily took a deep breath and then looked me square in the eye. "I wanted to tell you that I really liked helping Jessileigh today."

You wouldn't know it from the look on her face, but I waited her out to see if she had more to say.

"I never really tried to talk to her before. She never seemed to want to be anyone's friend. But today was really fun."

"She liked having you for a helper too," I said, and now I was the one mentally high-fiving myself.

"She did?" Lily asked, her eyes going big with wonder.

I nodded. "She sure did. Actually, she asked if you would maybe be her buddy during art tomorrow."

Lily's face was suddenly brighter, her smile lighting up her whole face. "I'd really like that, Mr. Curtis."

I nodded again. "Then it's settled. You are Jessileigh's official buddy."

Lily thanked me and turned to walk away. I thought that we were done, but she turned around again to face me. "Mr. Curtis?"

"Yeah?"

"Jessileigh seems sad."

The kid was definitely insightful. "She is."

"Is it because she doesn't have any friends?"

There was no easy way for me to answer that. "Maybe. Would you be sad if you didn't have any friends?"

She thought about that for a long moment before nodding. "I would."

"Maybe you could be Jessileigh's friend—and her buddy at school. What do you think?"

There was that smile again. "I hope she likes to play with dolls. I have lots of them. Do you think she does?"

It seemed logical. "Sure. What little girl wouldn't like to play with dolls?"

I could see Lily's mind going a million miles an hour. She turned to leave again only to turn around one more time. "Mr. Curtis?"

I tried to keep my frustration out of my tone. "Yeah?"

"Do you think tomorrow we can work on math first? You know, instead of having extra reading time?"

The kid had really pulled through for me today. How could I say no? "Yeah. I think we can definitely do math first."

"Yeah!" she cried. "Thank you, Mr. Curtis! Thank you!" Then before I knew it, she lunged her little body at me and hugged me before running from the room excitedly.

And damn if my heart didn't tug again.

I needed to get going. Suddenly it felt as if the walls were closing in on me. I did a quick cleanup and decided that it would have to do. I grabbed the books and folders I was going to need to work on and stalked out of the classroom.

And walked directly into Kristin.

"Oh!" she said as we collided.

I didn't have both hands free, thanks to the load of books I was carrying, but I did manage to steady her with at least one hand. "Sorry," I said a little distractedly.

"No, no... It was my fault," she said.

"Is everything all right?" There was no reason for her to be here, and at the moment, I wasn't sure I could even handle talking to her.

"I wanted to thank you. Lily just came down to my room and told me about what happened today. I know she's a little overwhelming at times and she's a stickler for the rules, but today you made her feel... special."

And there was that smile.

That beautiful damn smile that took the tug I felt earlier and turned it into a full-on squeeze.

"She's a great kid," I said, desperate to focus on something other than her smile, her lips, and how much I wanted to touch them, taste them. "I knew she'd be the perfect choice to help Jess."

"Well, whatever the reason, I want you to know that you made a real impression on her. All her teachers praise her for her work ethic. She's a good student. But no one has ever given her..." She paused. "Lily's like an old soul sometimes. And yet she's only six. So no one treats her like anything more than a six-year-old. Today you changed that."

Her eyes met mine, and I felt like I was drowning. Then her hand reached out and rested on my forearm—much like it had the other day—and the contact burned. I'm sure it was an innocent gesture, and there was nothing forward or coy about it. That wasn't who Kristin was. It was something—if I was being honest with myself—that I found oddly appealing. She didn't flirt. She didn't play games. The only one thinking about this touch as being more than a friendly gesture was me.

And now I wanted to touch her too.

And not so innocently.

For my own self-preservation, I stepped away. "Thanks," I mumbled, looking down at the ground. "I'm glad that she's happy about... you know. Anyway, I need to go. Have a good night."

And then like a coward, I turned and walked away.

And secretly hoped that this time Kristin watched me until I was out of sight.

5

KRISTIN

THE FOLLOWING DAY, I WAS FEELING RATHER FRAZZLED AS I walked outside to the after-school pick-up line. It wasn't my day to help with crowd control, but I wanted to catch Lily before her grandparents picked her up.

Nick's parents still lived here in town, and since he'd died, I'd done everything I could to make sure Lily continued to have a good relationship with them. She usually spent the afternoon with them once a week, coming home after dinner.

I found Lily in line with her class, talking to Jessileigh, a pretty classmate who always looked like a princess with her perfectly coifed hair and expensive clothes.

When she saw me, Lily smiled and reached her arms out for a hug.

"How was school today?" I asked after we'd pulled back from the hug.

"It was pretty good."

"Did you learn anything interesting?" I tried to keep the question discreet so it didn't appear to outside observers that I was poking around for information on Declan.

After yesterday, I'd half decided that there wasn't the cause for concern I'd originally thought, but I wasn't completely convinced yet, so I needed more information.

"We started with math, so that was good, but we didn't do very much. We finger-painted. Jessileigh was my partner for art." Lily looked up at me with big eyes. "Mr. Curtis tried a science experiment."

"Really?" I was surprised and somewhat relieved by this news—since it seemed like a sign that he was trying to take the classroom more seriously. Maybe things were really looking up. "What was the experiment?"

"He made parachutes for these little soldier men. It was supposed to show how the wider the cloth the slower they fell. That's the way the air works."

"That sounds fun. Did it work?"

Lily looked like she was almost smiling. "No. All the men fell down to the ground real fast."

"Very fast," Jessileigh said. She'd obviously been listening in, and now she stepped over. "One broke his leg. One broke his back. And the other broke his neck." She giggled. "It was funny. They all had to go to the hospital."

"Oh my." I wasn't sure even what to say to this, although I wanted to giggle too at the image of Declan dropping toy soldiers to the ground with parachutes that didn't work. "What did he say about why it didn't work?"

"He just said it was supposed to work," Lily answered, covering her mouth with her hand. "The air wasn't co-oprating today. I don't think he knew what was wrong."

I sighed. Of course he didn't know. Maybe he was trying a little more, but he still seemed completely clueless as a teacher. "Well, maybe he knew, but he wanted you all to figure it out."

Lily shook her head. "I don't think so. He was like you when you do bumper cars with me."

"What do you mean?"

"The way you pretend to have fun but really don't know how to move them good."

I smiled and kissed Lily on the cheek, feeling a wave of affection at the sight of her serious expression. "I'm not *that* bad at bumper cars."

Lily turned to the other girl. "Yes, she is."

I made a teasing face at my daughter and then said to the other girl, "Your name is Jessileigh, isn't it?"

"Yes. It's nice to meet you." The girl had surprisingly meticulous manners.

"It's nice to meet you too, Jessileigh." She was definitely not the normal kind of girl Lily gravitated toward as a friend.

For some reason I glanced across the yard and saw Declan standing on the outskirts. He was looking in our direction with a strange sort of focus.

It wasn't his day to do crowd control either, so I had no idea why he was just standing there watching, like he was ready to pounce or something.

The man was strange.

He was also so good-looking in the afternoon sun that I had to glance away before my mind went in wrong directions.

"Oh, there's your grandma and granddad, Lily. We'll see you later, Jessileigh."

I walked Lily to the front, where her grandparents were pulling up in the line of cars. The adults picking up children weren't supposed to get out of the car since it slowed down the line, but Nick's mother did anyway. She hugged Lily and then hugged me and then settled Lily in the back seat before she hugged me again, explaining that they were going to go to the zoo, which was having some sort of Christmas exhibit.

After I gave them a final wave, I also waved at Jessileigh, whose father had picked her up in a very expensive car.

Then I turned around to walk back inside, and my eyes met Declan's across the yard.

I was strangely unsettled by the look. I had no idea what it meant. And I definitely had no idea why I was suddenly picturing him looking at me that way in bed.

That idea was more than enough to completely rattle me, so I pushed it from my mind and instead thought about what Lily had said earlier.

Declan teaching was like me trying to do bumper cars. I always felt clueless and frustrated in bumper cars, and she'd evidently picked up the same thing from Declan in the classroom.

It was the final straw.

I really didn't want to tattle on another teacher, but I'd given him more than enough time to get it together and deal with any new-teacher adjustments.

This couldn't be normal adjustments to the classroom. He was genuinely unprepared to teach a first grade class, and Mrs. Bradbury wouldn't return from maternity leave for ten more weeks.

I had to say something to the principal. I couldn't just let something so important slide.

I was sure I was doing the right thing, but it left me feeling uncomfortable, so I killed some time, straightening up my classroom before I headed to Chuck's office.

He always had an open door for the hour after school ended for any teachers who had problems or concerns.

I had to wait for five minutes because he was talking to someone else, but then Rose waved me in.

"Hi, Chuck," I said with a smile, telling myself I really had no other choice than to do this.

"Kristin. I'm glad you came by. I was wanting to chat with you anyway. Have a seat."

"You were? What about?"

"Why don't we deal with your issue first." He was smiling, but there was a faint underlying awkwardness as if he were feeling as uncomfortable as I was.

I had no idea why he would be.

I cleared my throat. "Well, honestly, I hate to come to you like this, but I've tried handling it on my own, and it's just not working. Actually, I've tried multiple times to talk to him and can't get any answers out of him. I'm worried about Lily's substitute—Declan Curtis. He doesn't seem to know what he's doing in the classroom, and he won't give me any information on his background. I just don't understand why. It's strange. Like he's hiding something. I don't want to get him in trouble or anything, but I also don't want someone questionable to be teaching one of our classes." I took a deep breath and made myself calm down since saying it all out loud made me even more worried and frustrated.

"He hasn't been in the class for very long. Give him some time." Chuck sounded overly laid-back—too laid-back for it to be believable, given what I'd just said.

"I've given him a week and a half. Lily tells me every day what they do in class, and as far as I can tell, they aren't learning much of anything."

"That's not true. I've been in that class every day just to keep an eye on it. I know Lily is a smart girl with high expectations, but it's not been that different from most first grade classes."

I took another deep breath and looked at the floor again so I wouldn't get angry. "You're not in there all day though. And—"

"Kristin, don't worry about it. Even if he's not the best teacher in the world, he's not going to be in the classroom very long."

"But Eileen won't get back for two and a half months."

"But there's nothing saying he'll be the substitute for all that time."

I stared at Chuck, suddenly realizing that he knew something I didn't know. There was a secret here. He was hiding something. Was Declan just filling in until a more suitable substitute could take over? If so, why not just come out and say it? Why was everyone being so damn secretive?

Maybe it should have been a relief that Declan wasn't going to be the teacher for the whole three months, but I was more frustrated that something was going on here that involved my daughter's class, and I didn't know what it was.

"Kristin, please trust me," Chuck said as if he realized the conclusion I'd come to.

I swallowed hard. "Are you sure you know what you're doing, Chuck?"

He opened his mouth to reply but then closed it again as if he'd changed his mind. Then he said, more slowly, "I think so. Sometimes you choose the best option when none of them are great."

I thought about that for a minute, still staring at him.

That was as much as he was going to admit to me. I realized it now. But my blood was still pumping with anxious confusion. "If there's something going on that involves the children's welfare, then the parents need to know."

"I promise, Kristin. Lily is in absolutely no danger. The children are as safe right now as we can make them."

"Chuck..."

He sighed loudly but not with annoyance. "Declan

Curtis may not be an ideal teacher, but he's doing the best he can, and maybe we need to show him a little kindness and compassion instead of criticizing his every move."

Being that I knew I was the only one with an issue, I took it for the stern critique that it was.

I nodded, seeing he was confident about that at least. With a sigh, I got up. "Okay. I'll trust you for now since I have to. But I'm still going to keep an eye out." I gave him a helpless look. "My daughter's education is very important to me. So is the reputation of the school. I can't help but take things like this seriously and question things that don't seem right. I hope you understand."

"I do." He smiled and stood up too. "And I wouldn't expect anything else."

I did some prep work for tomorrow and, an hour later, was heading out to the staff parking lot.

It had been a long day, I was tired, and I was kind of looking forward to going home to an empty house where I could just collapse on the couch for an hour or so.

But as I approached my car—a sensible sedan—I realized that my couch time wasn't going to happen anytime soon.

One of the rear tires on my car was flat.

I slumped, staring at it, hoping it would miraculously reinflate while I watched.

No such luck.

I'd probably run over a nail or something. There was construction going on in our neighborhood. One of my neighbors had been complaining about nails on the road.

After a minute of just standing, I finally dropped my bag to the ground and opened my trunk. I did have a spare, so all I needed to do was put it on.

I could go inside and find someone to help me, but it would probably have to be Chuck, and he wasn't in any better shape than I was. Or I could call AAA and wait for an hour or more before someone came to change the tire for me.

Or I could do it myself.

I'd changed tires with Nick before, so I knew the process. With him being deployed, he'd made sure that I knew how to handle car maintenance and some of the basics that might need to be taken care of on my own. I could do it. I was sure I could do it.

This was just the first time that I had to do it.

Steeling my will, I hauled the spare out of the trunk and then found the small jack.

I wanted so much for Nick to be alive that I almost cried as I crouched down next to the flat tire to position the jack.

Then I remembered I'd better put the emergency brake on.

I was just standing up when a voice behind me said, "Did you piss off too many fourth graders, and one of them took revenge on your tire?"

I jerked in surprise and almost stumbled when I realized Declan was directly behind me.

He reached out, evidently to stabilize me, but his hands started on my shoulders and slid down to my waist. I knew it wasn't intentional—he was just instinctively trying to keep me from falling. But it felt like an embrace, and I reacted that way. I flushed and felt a shiver of excitement, brutally aware of his strong, warm body and the strength of his hands.

I pulled away, rather abruptly.

"Sorry," he said in a mild, teasing drawl. "I didn't really think it was a tire-destroying fourth grader."

"I know. You just startled me."

"Can I help?" he asked, eyeing the flat tire and the spare I'd pulled out.

"Oh. Yeah. I guess. If you don't mind." I felt rather befuddled, and unfortunately, I probably sounded that way.

"No problem at all."

"Thank you." I took the opportunity of leaning into the car to pull the emergency brake to pull myself together. This was ridiculous. I wasn't a naïve teenager who was into a boy for the first time. I was an adult. I'd already been married. I knew how to interact with a man without acting like a fool.

What the hell was wrong with me?

"I appreciate it," I added when he positioned the jack and started pumping it. "I think I could have done it, but it would have been a real pain."

"I don't mind." He grinned at me, looking amused but not flirtatious, which was a change from the way he'd smiled at me before. "Changing tires is my specialty."

He definitely knew what he was doing. He moved quickly and easily as he lifted the car on the jack, loosened the lug nuts, and pulled off the flat tire. He wore khakis and a short-sleeved shirt, even though it was December, and my eyes lingered on his well-developed biceps, his strong back, and his tight ass as he leaned over.

My mind went in very wrong directions, and there was no way I could rein it in, not until he secured the spare and lowered the car.

"Thank you," I said when he stood up.

"You're welcome." His eyes rested on my face, and I wasn't sure what to make of the expression. It wasn't that practiced flirtation I'd seen before, but it felt warm, admiring. It made a knot of excitement tighten in my gut. "My pleasure."

"I can't imagine that changing a tire is really a pleasure," I murmured, glancing down and then up at him again.

"I like to work with my hands."

A very particular feeling was coursing through my body now—one I hadn't experienced in ages. He'd stepped closer, and I couldn't look away from him. "I can see that." My voice broke slightly, so I cleared my throat. "It's nice to know that you're good at something."

I hadn't thought through those words either, and I realized they might have sounded meaner than I'd intended.

He didn't take them as mean though. His smile warmed even more, and he took another step toward me until he was only inches away. "I'm good at a lot of things."

"Like what?" I was breathless now, and my body seemed to know what was coming, even though my mind hadn't caught up.

"Like this."

I still hadn't processed exactly what was going on, so I wasn't prepared when he lifted one hand to cup my face and then leaned down to kiss me.

I gasped against his lips—from pleasure and excitement and surprise all at once—and my hands flew up instinctively to cling to his shirt. He made a little humming sound and pressed into me more, sliding his hand to the back of my head.

At first his lips just brushed against mine, but then I couldn't help but open to the kiss so his tongue could start to explore.

My mind roared with feeling and sensation as I eagerly responded. I couldn't help it. It felt so good, and it had been so long since I'd felt this way. I pressed my body against his and wrapped my arms around his neck.

A first kiss—so out of the blue like this—shouldn't have been so deep or lasted so long. But neither of us pulled away. I loved the tension I felt in his body and the shameless entitlement of his hands, one of which slipped down toward my bottom.

But this was a first kiss.

This was a new man.

The first man I'd kissed since…

Then suddenly I remembered Nick. And I remembered it was Declan I was kissing now.

And I remembered that I didn't even really like him. And that there was something secret going on.

I gasped again with dismay and jerked myself away from him.

We stood staring at each other, both of us panting, for a minute.

"What—?" I began but was incapable of finishing the question.

He looked rather dazed, as if the kiss had affected him just as much as me.

"I can't…" I broke off, suddenly desperate to escape from here, get away where I could think straight again. "I can't do this."

I found my keys and opened the driver's door of my car. "Thank you for helping me with my tire. But I can't do this."

I sounded shaky and thick, but there was no help for it. My body still buzzed with my response to that amazing kiss.

Declan still didn't say anything as I got quickly into the car and drove away.

He was still standing by himself in the parking lot as I turned the corner and lost sight of him.

6

DECLAN

NORMALLY I WAS ALL FOR KISSING A WOMAN AND LEAVING her a little dazed and, dare I say, dazzled. But what just happened here in the parking lot was on a completely different level.

I was the one left dazed.

And dazzled.

And confused as fucking hell.

I raked a hand through my hair and looked around to see if anyone else witnessed what happened because with the way Kristin lit out of here, I wasn't sure I didn't imagine it all.

Now, I was not completely clueless. From what I've gathered, Kristin Andrews wasn't in the habit of dating or getting involved with men since her husband died. As the town sweetheart, I imagined that most men were a little too intimidated to approach her. And no doubt she had perfected the back-off vibe like the one she'd been giving me for almost two weeks.

On top of that, she'd probably devoted her entire life to Lily, and I got that. I could appreciate that. What was bothering me was the fact that she pretty much took off and didn't even want to... I don't know... acknowledge what had just happened.

Sure, some could argue that it was just a kiss.

Right. And the *Mona Lisa* was just a painting.

No, what happened here was more than just a kiss. I had kissed my share of women—hell, more than my share of women—and none of them ever rocked me to the core the way Kristin just had. For a minute there I just about forgot my own name.

So now I was standing here like a schmuck in the middle of the school parking lot by myself with a raging hard-on, and there wasn't a damn thing I could do about it.

Well, there was. But what was I? A fucking teenager? Hell no.

With nothing left to do, I walked back into the school and grabbed the papers that I knew I was going to need for the weekend to grade and the lesson plans for next week. Maybe I'd be able to actually grasp some of it and get the kids to learn something.

Right. Like I was going to be able to make that happen.

I needed to focus. This was a multitasking job, and although my primary concern was Jessileigh, I also owed it to the rest of the kids to at least try to teach them something.

Shit. She'd really gotten into my head—Kristin, not Jessileigh. On every damn level. I wasn't overly concerned with doing any actual teaching when I'd started because I had a client to protect. But now, thanks to Kristin, I could see that I have an obligation to the rest of the class as well.

I was so taking a fucking vacation when this case was over.

With the classroom cleared up and my weekend homework packed up, I walked out of the school and back out to the parking lot. Was it really only minutes ago that I was standing out here and kissing Kristin—both of us acting as if our lives depended on it? I can tell you one thing, my sanity seemed to be depending on it.

By the time I was on the road and heading for home, my head was pounding and I could still feel her lips on mine. What the hell was happening to me? Women were never a real issue for me. When I was interested, I pursued. When I was done, I left. And the thing of it was, they all knew the score and nobody got hurt.

I had a gut feeling that it was not going to be like that with Kristin. For starters, she was completely different from any other woman I'd ever been interested in. She was... normal. I'm not saying that I date freaks or anything, but the women that I dated were less... encumbered. Kristin Andrews came with a fucking list of hang-ups and issues.

For starters, there was Lily. I'd never gotten involved with a single mom. I'd always enjoyed the freedom of dating women who were available at all times for whatever came up. Somehow I sincerely doubted that Kristin would be available for a midday quickie or a middle of the night hook-up if she had a kid to worry about.

Then there was the fact that she was a widow.

Shit.

I knew how I felt at having lost one of my best friends to combat. I couldn't even imagine how much harder it is to lose a spouse. A year later and I was still fucked-up over Gavin's death. For so many reasons. I knew the part I played in it, and it ate me alive when I let myself think about it.

And even when I didn't. Who am I kidding?

Survivor's guilt. That was what I keep hearing, but I knew better. It was that, but it was more. A million times since that day, I'd thought about how it should be Gavin living my life and how Gavin should be the one here for all the things that have happened since the rest of us came home. And every time I thought of it, I wondered how I could've been so damn careless to let it happen.

I was seriously contemplating going home and getting blind, stinking drunk when my phone rang. I saw Cole's number on the screen and hit the Bluetooth button. "Hey."

"Hey! How's school going? Did you finger-paint today?"

My jaw hurt from grinding my teeth while listening to him laugh. "You're a fucking riot. What do you want?"

"Ooo... someone's in a pissy mood. What's going on? Did you miss nap time?"

I was so kicking him in the throat when I saw him again. "Look, asshole, it's been a long day. Is there a reason for this call, or are you just being a douche for your own entertainment?"

"Well, I guess you're out of school today since you're using the bad words," Cole joked. "And actually, yes, there is a reason for this call."

"Then get to it."

"Seb called earlier and said that he did some major updates on our computer software. We did a conference call, but we knew you were still in school, so I volunteered to pass on the information."

"What does this mean to me? What kind of software?"

"It's for doing background checks and whatnot. The program that he has us using now offers more detailed reports faster. I know that you're on a case and already have your information and you know exactly who you're dealing with, but for future reference, there's now more tools for you to work with."

"Fine." I didn't really give a shit about computers and software or background checks right now. I just wanted to get home and have some peace and quiet and a shot or two of whiskey to take the edge off.

And then another two or three to make me forget.

"Great," Cole said and then paused. "Now that business is out of the way, why don't you tell me what's going on?"

"Nothing's going on. It's been a long week, and I'm not in the fucking mood for jokes."

"Okay," he said slowly. "So we won't joke."

"We?" I asked sarcastically.

"Okay, fine. I won't joke. What's going on? You sound

like you're pissed about something. Is the kid okay? Has the mother been a problem?"

"The kid's fine. The mother has been MIA since I arrived. I don't think it's on purpose—she doesn't even know about me. I think that she's biding her time right now since the judge ordered supervised visitation. If I'm reading the situation correctly, she's going to try to play nice for a little while, prove that she can be trusted, and wait for everyone to let their guard down."

"You think she's going to grab the kid?"

"I'm almost positive. From everything that I've learned about this woman, she's a little unstable. She may grab Jessileigh and manage to stay under the radar for a couple of days, but the call of the limelight is too great."

"So then what's the big deal? She grabs the kid, then fucks up, and you've got her on kidnapping. I'm still not seeing why we're even on this case."

I huffed loudly with agitation. "The big deal is that the entire thing can fuck up the kid's life. Her mother is unstable, and she's gotten abusive with her. I'm not willing to let an innocent child get beaten and emotionally brutalized on my watch!"

I didn't realize that I was shouting until Cole said, "All right... all right... Calm down."

I was way too close to the edge right now. There was too much going on, and my head was spinning.

"Seriously, Dec, you're sounding a little unhinged. Talk to me, man. What the fuck is going on over there?"

Out of the four of us, I never really confided much in

Cole. Levi was our rock. He kept us all grounded and somewhat in control. Sebastian was the supportive one. But Cole? Cole was a loose cannon most of the time. He'd had a rough life and pretty much anything that anyone was going through paled in comparison to the things he had survived before becoming a Marine.

"It's nothing, man. Don't worry about it. I'm just in a shitty mood because I hate playing teacher."

"Yeah, yeah, yeah. Tell that to someone who may actually believe you. There's more going on. What is it?"

I could simply hang up, or I could take my chances and deal with the razzing he'll no doubt give me when I'm done.

I took a deep breath. "Okay, so I kind of kissed one of the teachers." And then I waited.

And waited.

And waited.

"Was it a dude?" Cole asked.

I couldn't help but laugh. "No. It wasn't a dude. Kristin's a fourth grade teacher, and her daughter's in my class and..."

"What the hell's the matter with you?" Cole snapped. "You kissed one of the kid's moms? Who does that? Is she married?"

"No. No!" I said more adamantly. "Her husband died a couple of years ago. He was a SEAL." *Dammit.* "She's been dogging me since I arrived here and checking up on me, and I kind of thought she was a bitch but..."

"Just because she's hot doesn't mean she isn't a bitch."

"Shut the fuck up! You don't know what the hell you're talking about!"

"Ah... so it's like that, is it?"

"What? Like what?"

Cole growled with disgust. "I am getting so tired of you guys all doing this. It's bullshit."

"What the hell are you talking about?"

"Okay, let's backtrack for a minute. This woman..."

"Kristin," I reminded him.

"Yeah, whatever," Cole said dismissively. "Kristin's been watching you and ratting you out and whatnot, but you're attracted to her. Am I right so far?"

Unfortunately.

"I'll take your silence as a yes. So you're attracted to her and you kiss her. What's the problem then?"

"She took off as soon as it was over."

"Maybe she had someplace to be."

I shook my head even though Cole couldn't see it. "No. It was more than that. She was a little freaked out and just sort of took off and left me standing in the middle of the damn parking lot feeling more than a little shell-shocked."

"That good, huh?"

"I've got the whole weekend to drive and find you and kill you," I sneered. "Remember that."

"Yeah, I'm scared." Cole paused. "So what has you more freaked out—the fact that you kissed her and she took off or that you kissed her and it was more than just a kiss to you?"

"Shit," I muttered.

"Please, I'm the one sitting here playing Dr. Phil. You don't get to mutter anything."

"It... it felt like more. It wasn't a calculated thing. One minute we were talking and the next... I just had to kiss her. I know we were in the middle of the parking lot, and I know that she's a single mom and a widow and all that, but... I'm totally screwed here. I don't know anything about her, and she's not like any other woman I've ever pursued. I think I scared her off, and now I'm not going to know anything about her."

"Uh... that's not completely true."

"What do you mean?"

"New software? Hello? Do you not remember my reason for this call?"

"I bet you're sorry you volunteered to call me now, aren't you?"

Cole chuckled. "More than you know."

"So... what? I should investigate her a little? Is that what you're saying?"

"It can't hurt. Maybe if you know a little bit more about her, you'll have an idea of how you want to proceed and if you want to proceed. You may not find out everything that you want to know, but you may find out enough to decide what happens from here. Think about it."

How could I not?

Two hours later and my head was still spinning.

From everything that I could find, Kristin Andrews was your typical all-American girl. A do-gooder. Someone who played by the rules, paid her bills on time, and never had a speeding ticket. She was a local girl who married her high school sweetheart and was primed and ready to live a fairy-tale life complete with kids, a white picket fence, and living happily ever after.

And then her husband had died.

I read the news reports and even managed to find some military records that weren't out there for public knowledge. Nicholas Andrews was a SEAL and a damn good one. What had happened to him was an accident. Helicopter crash. No one to blame. No enemy fire.

No friend who was supposed to have his back fucking it up.

The guy had a damn-near perfect career record and had a beautiful wife and baby girl waiting for him to come home.

But he wasn't.

Sitting back, I scrubbed a weary hand over my face. Everything that I'd seen screams for me to back away. I was not the kind of guy who was looking for a family, a dog... a white picket fence. No, I was the guy that was always looking for a good time—no strings attached. Kristin Andrews screamed strings.

I scrolled through some pictures that were on file—pictures showing her before her husband was killed. Kristin as a cheerleader in high school and again as homecoming queen. Her wedding picture. Pictures of the two of them embracing when Nick had come home and seen Lily for the first time. And then her standing next to his casket when he'd been flown home. For the first time in my career, I felt like a voyeur. This felt wrong to be looking at them, and for a brief moment, I was overwhelmed with jealousy at seeing the two of them together.

I closed the on-screen file and turned away from the computer and felt sick to my stomach.

I knew what the right thing to do was.

I knew that I was the wrong man for someone like her and Lily.

And yet...I knew that it was going to be hard as hell to stay away. If she gave me even a hint of encouragement, I'd crumble.

I wasn't sure which option I was hoping for.

It was time for a drink.

Monday morning I was in the front office collecting some papers when Kristin walked in. I didn't have to even turn around to know it was her, I just... knew. I turned around and smiled at her and saw the horrified look on her face.

Not the most encouraging reaction a guy could hope for.

"Good morning," I said softly.

She gave me a curt nod but said nothing.

"Did you and Lily have a good weekend?"

She still said nothing. Without even a glance in my

direction, she grabbed the papers from her mailbox and turned to walk away. I was so stunned by her reaction that I stood there like a fucking mute myself until the door closed and I realized that she'd walked out. Hell no. This was so not the way it was going to go.

I walked out of the office and stalked after her. It was early enough—most of the teachers wouldn't be in for at least another fifteen minutes, and I knew for a fact that she let Lily hang out in her classroom until it was time for her to come down to class. If I was going to have a hope in hell of talking to her, I needed to grab her before she got close to her own room.

It didn't take long to see her walking down the hall, and I jogged after her. She nearly screamed when I jumped in front of her. Her beautiful eyes went wide.

"You nearly scared me to death!" she hissed quietly.

"Well, I wouldn't have had to do that if you'd just talked to me in the office."

She scowled. "I'm busy. I have things to do before the first bell. I don't have time to sit around and talk."

"Too bad. Either you give me five minutes of your time, or I'll follow you to your room while talking to myself—loudly—about what happened Friday afternoon." I saw her jaw drop slightly. "Who knows who'll be around to hear me?" I said with a shrug.

"Fine." She looked around and then turned and walked back to my classroom. I followed, and once inside, I shut the door. "Five minutes," she snapped.

"You know, some people might take your attitude as a

sign that you want nothing to do with them." I stepped closer to her. "I'm not one of them."

"Then you clearly don't know how to read people," she said defensively.

I was a fucking *pro* at reading people, and right now I could see the pulse at the base of her throat beating wildly. I heard the slight tremble in her voice.

I also heard her slight intake of breath when I took another step closer.

"I asked if you and Lily had a good weekend," I reminded her.

"Yes. It was fine."

"That's good. She'll be happy to know that we have big math plans this week in class."

Kristin visibly relaxed. She even almost smiled. "I'm sure she will."

I nodded. "Look, about... Friday..."

She held up a hand to stop me. "It was a mistake," she said quickly. "You took me by surprise. I... I don't date much... or at all, and let's just say that I was curious. It didn't mean anything. Really. I'm sorry that I took off the way I did, but I didn't want to... encourage you or give you the wrong idea. I'm not interested in dating—anyone." Her eyes met mine. "So really, let's just forget about it. It's not a big deal."

Not a big deal? Was she for real? I almost wanted to reach out and shake her. Or kiss her. I wanted her to admit that it meant something. That was way more than a curious kiss. It was more than casual. It was a kiss full of longing and promise and... dammit. I looked a little closer, and that's when it hit me.

She was scared.

The rapid pulse, the rapid speech... and she was fidgeting.

"I haven't kissed anyone since... Nick," she said quietly. "So I guess it was only natural for me to react the way I did."

"Kristin," I began just as softly. "I'm honored, then, that it was me you kissed." I ran a hand through my hair. "I know that you're scared." She made to interrupt, but I stopped her. "I'm scared too."

"You are?" she asked, her eyes wide.

I nodded. "I've never met anyone like you before. I'm no saint, Kristin. I usually take a very casual approach to relationships, but I look at you and it doesn't feel... casual."

"No. You can't. It can't," she said as she shook her head.

I closed the distance between us and placed a finger under her chin and forced her to look at me. "I want you to look me in the eye right now and tell me that the kiss meant nothing," I said quietly. "Then tell me that you don't want me to kiss you again."

Her eyes went wide first, and then they quickly darted down and looked at my lips. It didn't matter what she said. I had my answer.

"I...," she began and took a step back. "It meant..." The first bell of the day rang, and the moment was lost. "I need to go," she said and quickly turned for the door.

"Kristin," I called, and she looked over her shoulder at me.

"It was a big deal," I said, but I forced myself not to move toward her. "And it will happen again."

She fled the room before I could utter another word.

7

KRISTIN

I spent the next week increasingly tempted by Declan.

It sounds ridiculous—since I was a grown woman with a daughter, a career, and a lot more important things to think about than a hot guy.

But I still spent a lot of time thinking about this particular hot guy.

It would have been fine if he'd acted normal—or at least what I considered normal. But even when he wasn't talking to me, even when he was all the way down the hall from me, it still felt like he was coming on to me.

I don't know how the man did it—but even just glancing my way, he could somehow make me think about sex.

It was very distracting.

I hadn't had sex since Nick died, so maybe that was part of it. I was a normal woman with a normal sexual appetite, and it hadn't been fulfilled for a long time. That was probably the explanation for why I couldn't stop thinking about Declan and why my mind kept slipping down very dangerous paths.

I wasn't going to be stupid though. I had Lily, so I had to make good decisions—and starting a relationship with a man like Declan would never be a good decision.

I was reminding myself of this again—for the four hundredth time that week—as I walked toward the office before school to check my box.

Maybe I wouldn't see Declan today. Maybe I could have a break from resisting his hot eyes and sexy voice.

No such luck.

"Good morning," he said in that very sexy voice, as he fell in step with me in the hallway.

I took a deep breath and gave him a long-suffering look. "Good morning." I might have sounded a little prim, but it was one of my only defenses for how he made me feel.

If only I hadn't kissed him. It would have been so much easier if I hadn't known what his hands, his lips, his body felt like against mine.

No taking it back now.

He was giving me that half smile and sidelong look, and I just knew he was thinking about kissing me. Or doing something more.

And I was really curious about the something more.

"You look very teacher-ly today," he said, a faint edge of laughter in his tone.

I had to fight not to smile back since his expression was

contagious. "What does that mean?" I knew what he meant since I was wearing one of my teacher dresses—khaki with a red belt and even an apple pin that Lily had given me on my last birthday. And something in his eyes told me he was thinking about what it would be like to take the dress off me.

"That means you look so neat and proper that I feel compelled to see how hot and wild you are underneath."

I jerked to a stop and tried to look stern, although his words had conjured up a number of erotic visions that I really didn't need first thing in the morning. "I've told you that's never going to happen."

"I'm not prepared to accept that. I won't make another move on you unless you make it clear you want me to, but I'm not going to stop letting you know I'm interested."

"You should accept my answer and move on." I meant for my words to sound firm and convincing, but even I could tell that it was a half-hearted statement.

"You were the one who asked what I meant just now. What did you think I'd say?" He'd made no move closer to me and hadn't raised a hand to touch me, but his eyes never left my face, and they seemed to caress me with knowing entitlement.

It left me breathless. The man must be some sort of sex god to do this to me without even touching me.

"Don't act like this comes out of nowhere. You knew exactly what I was going to say just now. You wanted to hear it."

The husky edge to his tone sent a hot shiver down my

spine. I knew my cheeks were flushed, but there was nothing I could do about it. It was all I could do to cling to the strap of my bag so I wouldn't reach out to touch him.

His body seemed to radiate with a sensual energy I could hardly resist as we both stood in the middle of the hall.

"My answer is still no," I finally managed to say, my voice shakier than I wanted it to be.

He reined in the sexiness a touch as he gave me another dry smile. "Too bad." He didn't look discouraged or frustrated. He looked pleased with himself.

It made me very nervous.

I sucked in a deep breath as I made my way into the office, where Rose gave me a cheerful greeting. She greeted Declan as he came in after me, and—when she asked him how things were going—I was able to grab my mail and handouts out of my box and make a dash for the door.

"I'll see you later," Declan said, looking over his shoulder at me. The words, the tone, and his expression combined into a kind of promise.

My heart jumped quite irrationally, and I mumbled, "Yeah. See you later, Rose."

I tried to relax as I returned to my classroom and tried to calm my mind of the day.

One thing was certain. There was no way I was going to let Declan keep me from doing a good job with my class. There were a few times of the day when it was okay to indulge in those fluttery thoughts, but right now was not one of them.

After school ended that day, I was heading outside to find Lily, who always lined up with her class until I came to collect her.

I was passing her classroom when I heard voices, so I paused to look inside.

Declan was leaning against his desk, and Lily was sitting on a chair, leaning down and holding her ankle.

I stopped short and watched since the sight was so unexpected.

"How is it feeling?" Declan asked. He was focused on the girl and hadn't realized yet I was in the doorway.

"It hurts bad."

"You twisted it. Sometimes that hurts bad. The ice will help. Jessileigh and Miss Marks will be back soon with it. But I don't think your ankle is sprained or anything, so it will probably feel better soon." His voice was calm and no-nonsense but surprisingly gentle.

"Okay." She was frowning, but she wasn't close to tears —so her ankle must not be hurting too badly. My initial swell of worry at my baby being hurt subsided.

I was about to step inside the classroom when Lily said, "Don't tell Mommy."

Declan blinked in obvious surprise. "Why shouldn't I tell your Mommy?"

"I don't want her to worry about me."

"She'll know your ankle isn't hurt too bad, but it's her job to worry about you."

"She worries a lot."

"How do you know she worries?"

"Because her forehead gets these little lines. Right here." She gestured between her eyebrows. "When Daddy died, they were always there. Now only sometimes."

"Well..." He cleared his throat, obviously at a loss for what to say. "She loves you. We sometimes worry about people we love."

"Oh. Who do you worry about, Mr. Curtis?"

He opened his mouth and then shut it again, and there was the strangest expression on his face. Almost trapped. Almost guilty.

Lily seemed to instinctively know what his expression meant. She parted her lips and stared up at him with big blue eyes. "Don't you have someone to love, Mr. Curtis?"

For some reason—for no good reason—my throat was suddenly so tight I could barely breathe. The wave of tenderness overwhelmed me, and it wasn't just directed at Lily.

It was also directed at Declan. The tenderness I felt was for him too.

"Sure I do," he said with just a little gruffness. "I have my mom and dad. And I have my buddies."

"You don't have a lady?" Lily's characteristic earnest sweetness was evident, even in the quaint wording.

"No, I don't."

"Don't you want one?"

"I... don't know." He looked slightly awkward, but Lily seemed oblivious of this fact.

I wasn't though. He seemed vulnerable somehow. Emotionally vulnerable.

Which I hadn't really thought was like him.

"What about a little girl?" she asked, still holding on to her ankle. "Do you think you might want to be a daddy?"

"I... Maybe."

"Oh. My daddy is dead."

"I know he is, Lily."

"And my mommy worries a lot."

"I know she does."

"She's a really good mommy."

"I know she is." Declan wasn't looking at Lily now. He was looking at a spot across the room. But there was something on his face that made me absolutely sure that he was thinking about me.

And I just couldn't take any more. My knot in my throat was almost unbearable, and my vision blurred over with emotion. There was no good reason for me to react like this from overhearing such a little conversation, but I felt close to both of them, like I was connected to both of them—in a way I hadn't since Nick had died.

I escaped to the bathroom where I went into a stall and suppressed a few silent sobs. I wasn't really crying. Just an overflow of emotion.

It was silly. No reason for it at all.

All the conversation meant was that Declan was a decent guy, and he was being kind to my daughter. And Lily liked and trusted him.

That was good. And that was all it meant.

I'd mostly convinced myself of that fact by the time I stopped by the office the next day at lunchtime to ask Rose about the schedule for the Christmas pageant so I knew exactly how many minutes my class had for their parts.

After she gave me a printout of the schedule, she gave me a gleefully curious look. "So what's going on between you and Declan?" she asked in a low murmur. Chuck's door was closed, and no one else was around, but she obviously didn't want to be overheard.

"Nothing," I said in an equally quiet voice. "There's nothing going on between us."

"Don't give me that. Every day I sense more vibes between the two of you. This morning you could cut the sexual tension with a knife. The guy is obviously crazy about you. When he looks at you, it's like he wants to eat you alive." Rose didn't sound jealous or catty. She seemed genuinely interested and excited.

Since her expression appeared authentic, I didn't just shut her down. I murmured, "He might be interested, but nothing is going to come from it."

"Why not? The man is sex on a stick."

"I need more than sex, Rose."

"For a real relationship, sure. But who says you need a real relationship with Declan?"

I blinked. "What are you talking about? I'm not going to do anything stupid that might make it difficult for Lily.

You know that. I'm just not in the stage of life when I can be casual about relationships."

"Does he want a relationship?"

"I don't know. I doubt it. He seems more like a fling kind of guy."

"So have a fling with him. For God's sake, Kristin, it's a once-in-a-lifetime kind of deal. You just know that man knows his way around the bedroom. And really, what's wrong with a fling? No strings. No messiness afterward. Just great sex with a man who knows what he's doing."

"I told you, I can't be casual—"

"About relationships, I know. But why does it have to be a relationship. We're talking about a fling here. You need some sort of rebound guy after Nick anyway, and this would be perfect. People do it all the time. It wouldn't have any negative effects on Lily or anyone else. Just enjoy yourself. You deserve it, Kristin."

For some reason she was making sense. A lot of sense. I had never been the type of girl who had flings. I had always been the one who believed in fairytales and happily ever afters. But I learned the hard way that life isn't always like that. I did deserve to have some fun—to cut loose from this good-girl image I'd had my entire life.

It would be a one-time thing.

Maybe two.

I'd only been thinking in relationship terms about Declan, and obviously that would just be stupid. But a temporary physical thing. Hot sex with no strings. Was that really so out of the bounds of possibility?

I'm not sure I could have even let it cross my mind if I hadn't overheard that little conversation the previous day. But after seeing him like that, he didn't seem as distant and confident and untouchable as he had before.

I'd never be stupid enough to expect a relationship, but did that mean I couldn't have *anything*?

Rose smiled. She was still speaking very softly. "You work so hard, and you've had such a hard time for the past couple of years. Why can't you just have fun? For a little while. What would be so wrong about that?"

Nothing. Now that I was thinking about it, I couldn't think of anything that would be wrong with that. Declan obviously wanted sex. I wanted it too.

And thanks to him and that kiss, I needed it.

Desperately.

We were both adults. Both willing. We could be honest with each other about it just being a temporary, no-strings thing.

Surely that wouldn't hurt Lily. Surely I could have something for myself.

"I don't know," I said at last, suddenly feeling hot all over at the idea of sex with Declan being a real possibility. "I have to think about it."

"Don't think about too much. It defeats the purpose." Rose was grinning as I walked away, and I tried to push the idea from my mind so I could focus on the rest of the day.

I didn't entirely succeed.

This afternoon was Lily's time with Nick's parents, which seemed to be uncannily fortuitous. She would be gone until after dinner. I would be on my own.

I could do anything I wanted.

I said goodbye to her and made sure she got safely off with her grandparents. Then my eyes strayed to where Declan was walking back into the school building.

He'd been standing in the background again, just watching as the cars pulled up to pick up the children. I had no idea why he did that every day, but he did.

It wasn't something I was going to figure out now. Right now I had to decide whether to go through with the crazy, naughty idea I couldn't seem to shake.

I told myself I needed to think about it some more. I just wasn't an impulsive person. I was a careful person. I didn't make decisions without thinking them through enough.

I was reminding myself of all this as I made my way back to my classroom. At least it was supposed to be my classroom I was returning to.

Instead, I ended up standing in the doorway of Declan's.

He was in there, bending over to pick up some books from the floor. His tight butt was very nicely displayed in that position.

I swallowed hard, feeling a deep rising of excitement and anxiety both. What was I doing here?

Was I really the kind of person who would do this?

He straightened up and must have realized I was there

since he turned around abruptly. "Hey," he said, sounding both pleased and surprised. "Don't just stand in the doorway. Come on in."

I stepped in, trying to control my breathing and think of something—anything—to say.

"Did I do something wrong?" he asked. "I suppose Lily must have reported on me and you're here to lecture me." He didn't sound annoyed the way he had a couple of weeks ago when I'd come to see him to find out why he wasn't teaching very well. From what Lily said, he actually seemed to have gotten a little better, so maybe he was learning.

None of that was on my mind right now anyway. "No," I managed to say. "I'm not here to yell at you."

"Then why are you here?" Something had changed on his face, as if he'd seen something in mine. He stepped closer to me, his eyes lingering on my face, slipping down to my body before returning to meet my gaze again.

I swallowed hard. "I..."

He lifted a hand, like he would touch me, but then intentionally dropped it again. "You said your answer was no."

"I know I did." A hot excitement was shuddering through me, blurring my vision, roaring in my ears.

"Is your answer still no?" He eased a little closer until there was just a breath between us, but he still didn't touch me.

I raised a hand and touched his chest. It felt like

another person who was doing this thing. I could hardly believe it was me. "No. I changed my mind."

I heard a quick intake of breath and felt his body tense. "You changed your mind about what, Kristin?" His voice was careful, and it felt like he was holding himself back.

I didn't want him to hold back anymore. I wanted him to let go. "It has to just be a no-strings kind of thing. Just a fling. Nothing messy."

I couldn't believe these words were actually coming out of my mouth. I almost didn't recognize myself anymore. But maybe that was a good thing.

"I'm all for no mess. Why did you change your mind?"

"I was only thinking relationship, and I can't be in a relationship with you. But sex..." I took a shaky breath and smiled. "I can do that."

He made a choked sound and cupped my face with his hand, and his eyes went all hot.

"Lily is with her grandparents this afternoon," I added.

"Excellent timing." He leaned forward, but before he kissed me, he dropped his hand again and straightened up. "We sure as hell can't do this here."

"I know. Where should we go?"

"We can go to my place. I'm not far," he said, walking over to his desk to collect his stuff.

"Okay. Let me grab my bag, and I'll follow you over there."

And that was it. We were evidently doing this.

We were getting together for sex in the middle of the afternoon.

I'd never realized I was that kind of person before, and I was strangely excited that I was.

Declan had a suite at one of those extended-stay places. I thought it was a little strange. He might be new to town, but surely he'd want a more long-term living arrangement. The thought flickered through my mind as I parked next to him and then got out of my car, but after taking one look at his face, the idea disappeared completely.

He must be just as excited as I was if his expression was anything to go by.

He took my hand and walked quickly into the building and then down the hallway to his door.

As soon as he'd unlocked it, he grabbed me and pulled me in, pressing me back against the wall as he kicked the door shut.

Before I could even open my mouth to say a word, he was kissing me.

His kiss was hot and urgent and hungry, and I was immediately overwhelmed by it. My mouth opened to his as he pushed his body against mine and slid one of his hands down to cup my bottom.

My blood was pulsing intensely as our tongues tangled and dueled, as I reached up to twine my arms around his neck.

"Damn, you're gorgeous," he murmured, breaking the kiss briefly to reposition our bodies slightly. He was still holding me trapped against the wall, and I had no complaints in the world. "I've been thinking about doing this since the day I met you."

"Me too," I admitted, gasping as he unbuttoned my dress enough to slide his hand inside to cup my breast over my bra.

I arched against the wall as he fondled me and then dragged his head down into another kiss.

As we kissed, I could feel a pressure of arousal growing inside me until I was raising one leg to try to wrap it around his. This move was impeded by my skirt, and I groaned in frustration as the erotic urgency built inside me with no relief.

"Fuck," he gasped, breaking the kiss to mouth a line of kisses down my throat. "I can't remember the last time I was this turned on."

I could feel it in his body that he meant it. The hard bulge of his erection was pushing into my belly, and I loved the feel of it—that I could turn this man on so much. "Me too," I gasped, clawing at his shirt and trying once again to raise my leg.

This time Declan bunched up my skirt enough for me to wrap my leg around him and moaned as the position let me rub myself against his thigh.

"Damn, you're so hot." His voice was rough and low. "I knew you'd be hot like this."

"Please. I can't wait much longer." I didn't know what had gotten into me. I was never out of control this way. Never so vocal about what I wanted.

He stifled a moan and kissed me again. Then he kissed his way down to my breasts, making me cry out in pleasure as he nipped at one of my nipples. He didn't spend too long on them though. Instead, he ended up on his knees in front of me, pushing up my skirt.

I was panting desperately, staring down at this handsome, sexy man on his knees before me. I knew what he was going to do, and I could barely hold myself upright as he kissed his way up one of my thighs toward my panties.

My arousal was hot and wet, and soon he'd slid my panties down to bare it to his sight.

"Spread your legs, Kristin," he rasped as his mouth reached my center. His breath was hot, and it felt incredibly good. Arousing.

I adjusted my stance to make more room for him, sprawled against the wall, trying to keep my knees from buckling as he parted my flesh with his fingers and then started to work me over with his lips and tongue.

It felt so good, and I was so aroused I couldn't keep quiet. I clung to his head, holding it in position as he pleasured me.

He knew what he was doing. His touch was skillful and urgent both. I was making silly sounds of pleasure as an orgasm grew inside me, and I couldn't keep my hips from rocking, trying to feel even more.

I couldn't believe this was me—against the wall in a strange room with Declan on his knees, between my legs. It was so unexpected—and so overwhelming—that it made the physical sensations even more powerful.

I was crying out loudly, fisting both hands in his hair and with one leg hooked over his shoulder as my climax finally broke. The sensations filled me, took all of me, until I was left breathless and limp in their wake.

I wouldn't have been able to stay on my feet if Declan hadn't unhooked my leg and then held me as he stood up. He was flushed and panting, just like I was, but he still looked like he was on the edge of losing it.

I was on the edge of falling into a sated heap on the floor. I gasped against his chest as both his arms went around me. "Thank you," I managed to say.

"You're welcome." He gave me a light kiss, and I could sense how much urgency he was now reining in.

I slid my hand down to the bulge at the front of his pants. "Now maybe we can do a little something for you."

8

DECLAN

It's safe to say that I was an arrogant son of a bitch most of the time. I took what I wanted, when I wanted it, and I was good at what I did—no matter what it was. Some would call me selfish. Some would comment on how huge my ego was. I had enough confidence for three men.

Here I was after messing up the sweet girl next door, and she looked hotter than anything I'd ever seen. Her dress was bunched up to her waist, and her panties were gone, and she was panting after an orgasm that I gave her. There was a primal part of me that wanted to pound my chest with pride at what I'd just done.

I made the good girl misbehave in the sexiest of ways.

Right now Kristin's hand was stroking my arousal through my pants, and as much as I was enjoying it—hell, who am I kidding, I was loving it—I was nervous.

Actually, I was as nervous as a virgin on prom night.

That was not what I was expecting to feel at all.

I knew that she hadn't been with anyone since her husband died, and I had a pretty good feeling that she hadn't dated much—if at all—before she married him. That was a lot of pressure on me.

Normally, with the women I get involved with, I was not overly concerned about my performance. I'd been told more than enough times that I was good in bed, and I knew how to give a woman as many orgasms as she could stand. But Kristin? I was torn about what to do.

I didn't want to be aggressive with her and scare her off. Even though I was about ready to burst from the touch of her hand—and she hadn't even gotten to the skin-on-skin contact yet. I could go slow and gentle—but I didn't know if I was capable of that right now. I'd wanted her for what seemed like forever, and all I wanted was to get us both naked and be buried inside her.

"You're thinking awful hard over there," she said as she leaned in and ran her tongue across my lips.

I was in deep trouble.

I wanted this to be good for her. I wanted this to be something that she wasn't going to regret.

I certainly didn't want a repeat of her running away from me like she had after we kissed in the parking lot.

"I won't break," she whispered.

And all bets were off.

Quickly I removed her hand from the front of my pants and pinned her arms above her head against the wall. I dove in and kissed her, devoured her. She whimpered against my mouth, and I swallowed the sound.

With one hand holding her in place, I let my other hand begin to roam her body.

And what a body it was.

She was soft and curvy and so responsive to my touch that I was slowly going insane. Her dress was awkwardly bunched up, and the only thought going through my brain was that I had to get it off her. I had to get her naked. I had to see if she was as soft all over as I had imagined.

In a flash, I released her arms and cupped her bottom. "Wrap your legs around me," I growled, and she immediately complied. I walked us over to the bed and laid her down. With her hair splayed out against the comforter and her dress a tangled mess around her middle, she was the sexiest thing I had ever seen.

I pulled my shirt off and tossed it to the floor and kicked off my shoes. "Take your dress off."

Kristin's eyes went wide for a moment, and I cursed myself. Maybe I was pushing her too far, too fast. I was just about to apologize, to lean down and help her undress when she came to her feet in front of me. With those beautiful eyes never leaving mine, she unbuttoned, unbelted, and shimmied out of her dress.

And my heart just about stopped.

She was perfect. Kristin Andrews was my every fantasy come to life. It was like having my own centerfold model right in front of me.

I was never going to be able to look at her in one of her prim teacher dresses the same way again.

Standing there in scraps of white lace, she was a dream.

The white lace really played into the whole good-girl fantasy I'd built up of her in my head. And now that she was standing here in front of me in the flesh, I was afraid to even blink. My hands were actually shaking as I slowly reached out to touch her. My fingers skimmed over her face, her throat, her shoulders, her breasts.

"Declan," she sighed, and I replaced my hands with my mouth. I teased and suckled her through her bra until she was shaking and panting and trying to pull me down on the bed with her.

It would have been so easy to just follow her down, kick my pants off, and give us what we both wanted, but I wanted to savor this. I wanted to make it right for her. I know that we said that this was just... casual... but right now it felt like a hell of a lot more. I had no idea how much time we had—when she'd have to get back to Lily—but I needed this to be right. To be perfect.

To be everything.

Kristin pulled free of my arms and sat down on the edge of the bed and then scooted back until her head was on the pillows. She opened her arms to me, and I felt so damn humbled that I couldn't move for a minute. This beautiful, brave woman wanted me.

Me.

My conscience was pulling at me to do the right thing —be careful with her—and if I couldn't, to just walk away.

Fuck my conscience.

She licked her lips as her sensual gaze met mine, and I saw in those eyes that she wanted this just as badly as I did.

"You're too far away," she whispered.

Now. It had to be now. Without breaking eye contact, I pulled my wallet out of my back pocket and took a condom out. Kristin arched a brow at me, and I smiled wickedly at her. "It pays to be prepared."

And then my pants, my socks, my boxer briefs were gone and I was slowly covering her body with mine. The skin-on-skin contact was intense—we both sighed at it—and then I was kissing her again as if my life depended on it.

She clung to me, her nails raked down my back, and I was damn near shaking with anticipation. I was just about to raise my head to look at her when she wrapped her legs around my waist, and it felt... perfect.

Somehow I managed to get that sexy-as-hell bra off her and tossed it to the floor to join where I'd dropped her panties earlier. I pulled back long enough to roll the condom on, and I saw a wide range of emotions cross her face—anticipation, desire... and uncertainty.

That one stopped me dead in my tracks. "It's not too late to change your mind," I said softly, even though my body wasn't quite on board with that option.

She shook her head. "No. I want this. I want... you."

Honestly, I should have just listened to her words. But I couldn't. Instead, I studied her face—her beautiful face—until she started squirm. Reaching up, I caressed her cheek. "Kristin, I want you to be sure. I don't want you having any regrets."

And that last comment was as much for her as it was for me.

Like I said, I don't think I could stand it if she ran away again and looked at me with the same aversion she had after the parking lot incident. Not only did that mess with my head, but it messed with my heart in a way nothing ever had before.

Her hands were roaming over my shoulders, my chest. Then she reached around and grabbed my ass and gently pulled me toward her—with a very sexy smile on her face.

And I knew right then and there that I would never tire of looking at her.

This wasn't casual.

This wasn't just sex.

"Declan," she moaned, arching up toward me.

And then I was slowly sinking into her, inch by inch. She sighed. She purred. She all but destroyed me. Her legs wrapped around me again, and I waited a minute for her to adjust to me. I kissed her gently on her lips, her eyes. "Tell me if I do something that you don't like."

Reaching up, she cupped my face in her hands. "I don't like that you're not moving."

It was like waving the checkered flag in my face. My hands found hers and pinned her arms above her head as I began to move. Slowly. "Like this?"

She shook her head.

I rocked a little harder into her, a little faster. "How about this?"

She shook her head again and seemed to be getting lost in the same sensations I was feeling.

"Tell me," I urged, unable to stop myself from moving harder and faster.

"Like that," she whispered. "Hard. I need it harder."

I gave her exactly what she wanted—what we both wanted—and soon she was writhing beneath me, chanting my name. "Please!" she said. And then she was pulling her hands free of mind and pulling me closer as she came—hard. Her tight channel clenching around me and her body wrapped around me, it was like nothing I had ever felt before.

She consumed me until it was impossible to tell where one of us ended and the other began.

"I can't hold back," I said hoarsely. "I need... I need to..."

"Yes," she cried. "Do it, Declan! Now!"

My orgasm hit me hard and fast—too fast for my liking. Over and over, my body shuddered and shook as it felt like everything I had emptied into Kristin.

Our breathing was heavy as I rested my forehead against hers. "I'm sorry," I said when I was finally able to breathe.

"For what?"

"I wanted to go slow with you. I wanted this to last longer." I raised my head and looked down into her eyes. "I wanted it to be perfect for you."

I realized what I was saying and suddenly panicked. We said this was a fling—possibly only a onetime thing. Well, that's what she said she wanted it to be. I never actually agreed to that. At the time, it seemed safe. It meant I'd finally get to feel her, taste her, make her mine. But now? It was a completely different story, and I was thinking in terms I'd never thought of before. Why was I getting so... I don't know... emotional about it?

It was more than a little unnerving.

Kristin smiled slowly at me. "It was perfect. Exactly what I wanted." She shifted slightly beneath me, and I gathered her into my arms as I rolled off her and tucked her into my side.

A million thoughts raced through my head—was she all right? Did she regret what we'd just done? Was she going to get up and get dressed and leave? Was this it? Was she disappointed in the whole experience and ready to go back to being co-workers and nothing else? Part of me wanted to know, but the other part was afraid of her answer.

"You're doing it again," she said.

"What?"

"Thinking too hard." She raised her head and looked at me, uncertainty written all over her face. "It's... it's been a long time for me. I'm sorry if I wasn't..."

I placed a finger over her lips to immediately silence her. How could she possibly be doubting herself? "There is nothing that you have to apologize to me for." My hands skimmed her face. "You were better than my fantasies."

Her eyes went wide. "Really?"

I nodded. "Really. And I've had some pretty vivid fantasies about you."

She blushed. "I... I've thought about you too."

I couldn't help but grin. "Yeah?"

She nodded. And blushed. That gave me a pretty good idea that her thoughts weren't of the G-rated variety.

"Tell me," I urged, my voice a little gruff.

Kristin ducked her head, and I could see her blushing. Unable to help myself, I tucked a finger under her chin and gently urged her to look at me. "Want me to tell you about mine first?"

She nodded.

My hand skimmed from her chin around to her nape and gently anchored there. "I thought about you wearing one of your prim and proper dresses—like the one you wore today—and stripping you out of it."

The shy smile she gave me at that admission told me she liked what she was hearing.

"I kind of like the idea of taking you from that sweet and innocent look to naked and panting my name," I said as I pulled her head down for a kiss. I meant to only give her a soft kiss, but she wasn't having that.

I kind of loved how she had a bit of a wild side and that I was the only one who was getting to see it.

When she lifted her head, she asked, "What else?"

"I think it's your turn to tell me what you've been thinking."

But she shook her head. She wasn't ready to.

Which was fine. I had no problem talking about all the naughty things I'd been thinking. With every scenario I described for her, her blush deepened and her breath quickened. When I mentioned how I envisioned taking her in one of the supply closets at school, she leaned down and silenced me with a kiss that was hot and wet and full of promise. And when we both came up for air, she was smiling.

Really smiling.

In that moment, I felt like I was on top of the world. "Kristin... it's not just—" I stopped, sort of faltered with my words. "I mean, I don't just think of you like this." Oh God. She's going to think I'm an idiot. "I like talking with you, spending time with you. Does that make sense?"

In my entire life, well, actually since I began dating at the age of thirteen, I never talked—or felt—like this with a woman. This was more than physical, more than just sex, and I wanted—needed—her to know that.

Slowly Kristin nodded. "I don't think..."

I knew what was coming. Feared it. I placed a finger over her lips again to stop it. "Don't," I said softly. "I don't want you to make up any excuses for how you feel. It's okay if you don't feel the same way. I just wanted you to know... I wanted to be honest with you."

"Declan," she whispered as her eyes scanned my face, "being with you... like this or even just around school, it... it scares me a little."

"I'm sorry if I came on too strong."

"No, no, it's not that," she said and then chuckled.

"Although you do get points for persistence." She paused, and her expression turned serious. "You bring out a side of me that I never knew existed. You've brought these... feelings out of me that I thought were gone." Her hand reached out and skimmed down my chest, her eyes following the progress before meeting mine again. "Sometimes just thinking of you makes me ache with need."

And just like that I was hard again. "I know you don't have a lot of time but..."

"It's okay," she interrupted. "I want you again too."

We kissed, and I knew that this time we'd go slowly. We'd explore.

And I also knew that this one afternoon wasn't going to be enough.

I was distracted to say the least on Monday when we were back at school. I had already known that we wouldn't see each other over the weekend, but once I walked into the building Monday morning, all I could think about was seeing Kristin.

Totally out of character for me.

By all accounts and purposes, I should have been done. I had pursued, I had captured, and I'd rocked both our worlds. But for some reason it wasn't enough. I wanted more. I knew it Friday, but I thought once the sexual haze was over and Kristin left my hotel room, that I would get my head together and realize that it was just sex.

Just a fling.

Even in the midst of it, I was telling myself it was more. But later on when I was alone, I tried to convince myself I was just caught up in the moment. That there was no way I was falling that hard, that fast. No way. So I tried to make light of it in my mind the next day, like it was no big deal.

That I could meet her on her terms and keep this as just physical. Just sex.

Just a fling.

My stomach sank when I realized it was more than that. Much, much more than that. Shit.

I lingered at the front office in hopes of running into her. I chatted with Rose and spent a few minutes with Chuck when Kristin finally walked in. She blushed furiously when she spotted me and wouldn't look at me directly.

Uh-oh.

I excused myself and followed her when she walked out the door. "Hey," I said, jogging to catch up with her. "How was your weekend?"

"Fine. It... it was fine."

My eyes narrowed a little bit as I fell in step beside her. "That's good. How's Lily? Did she have fun with her grandparents?"

She nodded.

I quickly maneuvered so I was in front of her, and she walked right into me. Her eyes were huge as she looked up at me. "What's going on?" I asked.

"What do you mean?"

"I mean..." I looked around to make sure no one was near us. "You're giving me the cold shoulder, and I don't know why."

"You're being ridiculous."

"Am I?"

She rolled her eyes. "Look, it's Monday. I've got a busy day. We have to start the kids rehearsing for the Christmas pageant, and I've got to focus on that."

I might have believed her if she had looked at me while she spoke. I tucked a finger under her chin and forced her to look at me. "I just wanted to make sure that you were okay," I said softly.

"I... I'm fine," she said. "I'm just not comfortable... with this."

"With what? Knowing that I'd like nothing more than to drag you into my classroom, lock the door, and fuck you senseless up against the wall?" My words were whispered in her ear, and she slowly relaxed against me.

She nodded. "I'd go willingly if I thought we wouldn't get caught."

I chuckled. "Now I'm not comfortable." She looked up at me, and I pulled her close—close enough so she could feel my erection against her belly. Her mouth formed a perfect O, and I smiled. "God, I want to kiss you right now."

"We can't."

"I know." That didn't make it any better. "Promise me something?"

"What?"

"That Friday wasn't it. That it wasn't a one-time thing?"

Who the hell was I? Was I seriously asking her for more? Me? The guy who never was the one who looked for more than a woman was willing to give?

"I... I don't know, Declan. I've got a lot on my plate, and I have Lily to consider."

"Promise me you'll think about it then."

Her eyes looked a little uncertain when they met mine. "I will."

And then I stepped aside and let her go.

For now.

Christmas pageants are their own personal form of hell.

This was a fairly small school, but you still had over a hundred kids that you had to corral into the auditorium and figure out who needed to stand where and when and then how to move everyone without it being too distracting.

I wish my drill sergeant was here. He'd know how to get those kids to listen and stay in their spots. It was exhausting.

My class was going to be sitting next to Kristin's class, but right now no one was sitting. The kids took this opportunity to start to run around like little hellions. I whistled loudly for my kids to line up so I could get a head count and get them seated.

"Twenty, twenty-one, twenty-two," I counted and felt a sense of panic. Someone was missing. No, two someone's were missing. Quickly I started moving the kids along into their rows and mentally checking my class list to figure out who wasn't there.

My stomach sank.

Jessileigh.

Shit! I had turned my back for a minute to see what was going on up on the stage and listening to Mrs. Crandall, the music director, give us all instructions, and now Jessileigh was missing.

"Everyone needs to stay in their seats. Understand?" I admonished my class and then began to frantically scan all the rows for Jessileigh.

"Declan? Is everything all right?" Kristin asked worriedly. She was standing beside me, and I'd never heard her approach.

"No," I snapped. "One of my kids isn't here. Actually, two of them…" I kept scanning the area. It shouldn't be this hard to keep track of these kids! How could I have let her out of my sight? She was my responsibility!

"It's okay. It's easy for you to lose sight of them in a situation like this. I'm sure…"

"You don't get it!" I said, unable to hide my frustration. "They are my responsibility. It's up to me to keep them safe, and if I don't do that, someone will get hurt!"

She took a step back and studied me.

"Jessileigh!" I called out.

"Yes, Mr. Curtis?"

My head snapped around as Jessileigh—and Lily—popped up behind the back row of seats. I stormed toward them and took a minute to rein myself in. "Are you supposed to be back here by yourselves, or are you supposed to stay with the group?"

"With the group," they both mumbled.

Taking each of them by the hand, I led them to our section and sat them on the end where I could keep an eye on them.

"Declan?"

Shit. Kristin was standing right there, questions written all over her face.

"Can I talk to you for a minute?"

I didn't want to be too far away from the kids, so I walked back a couple of rows but made sure I was facing them. Watching them. "What?" I snapped, my heart still racing at the thought of what could have happened.

"What just happened back there?"

"They wandered off and were hiding. I told them to stay with the group."

She shook her head. "It's more than that. You said that someone would get hurt. What's going on?"

A scrubbed a weary hand over my face and knew that she had a right to know what was going on. "Look," I began and knew that this had the potential to fuck things up royally between us. "What I'm about to tell you cannot go any further than between you and me. Do you understand?"

She nodded, her expression more than a little wary.

"I'm not a teacher..."

"I knew it!"

"Yeah, great. Save your pat on the back, Nancy Drew, until I'm done," I grumbled. "Anyway, I'm... I'm a bodyguard. Jessileigh's my client."

Kristin looked at me and then Jess and then back again. "I... I don't understand."

"Her parents are in a bitter custody battle, and right now there's a very real possibility that her mother is going to try to snatch her up and take her away. I'm here to make sure that doesn't happen."

"But she's her mother!"

I shook my head. "It doesn't matter. She's unstable, and there's been allegations of abuse."

"Maybe they're untrue," she said defensively.

I shook my head again. "It's been witnessed. And documented. Hell, she's all but admitted that if given the opportunity, she'd snatch the kid up just to piss her ex off. She's not allowed unsupervised visits with Jessileigh, but she's threatened to take her repeatedly. I'm here to make sure that doesn't happen. I'm here to protect her."

She went silent for a long moment. "So... so do you do this sort of thing a lot? Protect kids?"

"No. Jess is the first child client I've had. Normally it's a bit more... intense."

"You mean dangerous."

"Yes." I stared her down and watched her face. I knew the instant that it all registered with her and when she started to think of a way out of what we had begun. I could read her like a book.

"I see."

"No, you don't." I had to do something, say something quick. "Not all cases are dangerous," I said a little too defensively. "I have three partners and we trade off and..."

Looking around the auditorium, I could see her looking for an escape. "I... I can't deal with this right now, Declan. It's all just a little too much."

I knew it would be. "You can ask me anything you want about my job, Kristin, and I'll answer you. But you need to keep this to yourself. No one—other than Chuck—knows why I'm really here. I need to know that you're not going to freak out and say something."

She shook her head. "I won't." She looked over her shoulder toward Lily and Jessileigh. "Is she all right?"

"She's going to be," I said quietly. "I'll make sure of it. And Lily is perfectly safe too. I don't want you to worry about that."

With a curt nod, she turned and walked away, and I had a sinking feeling that this subject was far from over.

But we possibly were.

9

KRISTIN

I SPENT THE ENTIRE WEEK IN AN EMOTIONAL FURY—TORN between excitement over this new thing that had developed with Declan, confusion about whether I should have gotten into it at all, and worry about his admission of his real job and purpose here.

I'd always known he couldn't really be a teacher, but I'd never expected him to work in security and close protection. It fit him better, like he'd finally put on the right-sized outfit in my mind, but the fact that his job was dangerous was like a blaring warning siren in my head.

Nick's job had been dangerous, and he'd been killed. I wasn't about to risk something like that happening again to Lily and me.

All through the day, though, I kept telling myself it didn't matter. Declan and I had been very clear and open about things from the beginning. It was just a fling. Nothing serious. Nothing to get all uptight about.

Sex was sex. And sex with Declan might have been mind-blowing (I flushed hot just remembering it), but it was still sex. It didn't have to—it *wouldn't*—change my life.

I was mature and reasonable enough to have sex without assuming it would turn into love. And I was intelligent enough to know that I could separate the two.

Declan wasn't a man I could ever fall in love with.

My teaching all day was a little frazzled. A few times I actually forgot what I was talking about, and my students all giggled when I admitted it. It was ridiculous. Focus was something I'd always been good at, and it was just annoying that Declan had somehow managed to take that away from me.

I kept hearing his voice though. *Promise me that Friday night wasn't a onetime thing.*

I didn't want it to be. I was dying to have sex with him again, but first I had to assure myself that I was able to handle it without my whole life spinning out of control.

After school on Thursday, I was doing some lesson prep that I'd let slide for the past couple of days, while Lily read quietly in the corner of my classroom. I stared down at the math book and instead of equations, I pictured myself showing up at Declan's place later tonight. After Lily went to bed, I could get my elderly neighbor to sit with her. Then I could just go over there. Tell him it had to be casual, no strings attached. Then he would take me to bed.

I desperately wanted to be with him again. I'd only

seen him in passing today, but his eyes were speaking. I could read the expression clearly.

He wanted to be with me again too.

I took a long, slow breath and tried to think through the idea reasonably.

"Mommy," Lily said from her corner.

"Yes, sweetheart." I didn't look up from the textbook since I felt like I'd been caught, like I shouldn't have been having such thoughts in the presence of my daughter.

"Is there a blanket I can use?"

"What?" I looked up then and saw that Lily was on the floor. She must have found the pretty, plastic Christmas plates and teacups I'd bought for a birthday party in my class last week. There were some leftovers, so I'd put them in the cupboard. She'd laid out four place settings and was busily folding the napkins.

"I want a blanket so I can have a Christmas tea-party picnic. Is that okay?" She looked up at me soberly.

"Of course it's okay." I'd never seen her try to do a tea party before, but I was always quick to encourage her when she wanted to play. She was so focused on reading and school that I was glad whenever she did some sort of whimsical fun.

"Like in *Alice in Wonderland*," she added. "But it will be better with a blanket to spread it out on."

"Sure." I got up and went to the closet and pulled out an old quilt I'd used for some activity last year. Then I helped Lily spread it out on the floor and watched as she carefully arranged the place settings on it. I couldn't help but smile when she went to get the fake mini-Christmas tree I'd set up on a windowsill and placed it like a centerpiece.

When I saw she was having fun, I started to go back to my desk to finish my work.

"Will you have the tea party with me?" she asked, settling herself down cross-legged in front of one of the settings. "You can be the March Hare."

I chuckled and came back over. I really should work on those lesson plans, but Lily wanted to play like this so seldom that I couldn't say no. I lowered myself to the floor, trying to tuck my skirt around my legs so nothing inappropriate was showing. "I'll be happy to be the March Hare. Will you be Alice?"

"Of course." She reached up and pulled the elastics out of her ponytails, smoothing down her dark hair. "Alice doesn't wear ponytails."

"That's right. You look like the perfect Alice now. We'll have to imagine the Mad Hatter, but maybe you could talk for him."

"Yes, I can—" She broke off, her eyes darting over to the door of the classroom. "Hello, Mr. Curtis. Do you want to be the Mad Hatter?"

I gasped and whirled around to see that Declan was standing in the doorway, watching us with a half smile that looked both astonished and amused.

He stepped into the room. "I didn't mean to interrupt. I can see you're busy." His smile warmed as he looked from me to Lily.

Lily beamed at him. "You're not interrupting. We needed a Mad Hatter anyway."

"I'm supposed to be the Mad Hatter?" He looked particularly sexy and masculine, standing over us in his khakis and black shirt, with a slight stubble on his strong jaw. He didn't look at all like the kind of man who would be comfortable having a tea party or want to play a silly, girlish game.

"Yes, please. You can sit right here, and I'll pour you some tea." She patted the bottle of water she must have taken from my bag earlier, the only beverage the room offered.

"I'm sure Mr. Curtis is busy, Lily," I said softly. "He probably has a lot of work today, and we have to be considerate and not assume other people can always drop everything to play with us."

Lily blinked. "Oh." She turned her eyes up to Declan. "I'm sorry, Mr. Curtis. I am considerate. If you're too busy to be the Mad Hatter, I understand."

It was so sweet my chest ached. The poor little thing had lost her father, and she wanted so little. But Declan was simply not a man she could—or should—put her faith in.

He hesitated. I could tell he felt rather uncomfortable, as if he were being stretched in a way he just wasn't used to. I assumed he'd take the out I gave him and make a quick escape. Instead, though, he smiled again and lowered himself to the floor to sit in front of one of the place settings. "I guess I'm not too busy to have tea with two pretty ladies."

Lily's face broke out in a wide smile, and she started to pour the water into the teacups, giving us instructions on our roles and how we should act to be in character.

I tried to play my part as required, but my eyes and thoughts kept straying to Declan. He was taking his Mad Hatter character seriously although he obviously wasn't very familiar with the story. And I couldn't help but be touched as I listened to Lily give him instructions and watched him respond with a kind of gentle generosity I hadn't expected to see in him.

"We need to switch places," Lily announced without warning.

Declan had been pretending to drink tea out of his pretty little teacup, and he stopped with it perched at his lips. "Why do we switch places?"

"Just because. That's what they do. Right, Mommy?"

I was already getting up. "Right. That's what they do."

I felt Declan's eyes on me as I straightened my skirt, hoping again that nothing inappropriate was showing.

"Now you sit there, Mad Hatter," Lily directed, pointing at the place she'd just been sitting. "And, March Hare, you can sit there."

So we all took our new seats, and I tried not to giggle at Declan's expression. He clearly hadn't expected to partake in a tea party when he'd dropped by the classroom just now.

Lily seemed very pleased with the entire arrangement, and she told Declan, "Now you have to tell a poem."

He swallowed visibly. "What? A poem? Why?"

"That's what the Mad Hatter does, right? He says silly poems." She gazed at Declan expectantly.

He was clearly put on the spot, and for a moment I thought he might just get up to leave. After all, it wasn't like Lily was important to him.

Or that this was a scenario he was comfortable with.

But he didn't get up or make up an excuse. He cleared his throat and put down his teacup. "A poem. Okay. Uh, okay. *There was an old man from Nantucket.*"

I almost choked on my fake tea at the first poem that had evidently popped into his head.

Declan's eyes widened as he must have realized the rest of the poem he'd started to say. He looked from me to Lily quickly.

"That was good!" Lily leaned forward. "What's the rest of it?"

She was so innocent, and Declan was so visibly awkward that I had to raise my hand to cover my mouth to hide my smile.

He seemed to realize my suppressed humor and shot me a dark look that made me want to laugh even more.

"Go on, Mr. Curtis!"

He cleared his throat again. "Uh, right. *There was an old man from Nantucket. He, uh, had a really nice bucket.*"

I was having such a hard time not laughing now that I was trembling with it.

"Shh, Mommy," Lily hissed. "He's saying his poem."

"Right. Carry on."

That got me another dark look from Declan, who manfully and stiltingly proceeded. *"The bucket was red. And, um, he put it on his head. And... and... sometimes under his chin he would tuck it."*

I was gasping with laughter at the end of his improvised limerick, and Lily burst into loud applause that spilled over into giggles.

Declan soon was laughing too, and he could barely keep his composure as Lily demanded that he recite his fun poem again until she had memorized it and could recite it too.

I met Declan's eyes over the blanket, place settings, and mini-Christmas tree, and we shared a look of warmth and complete understanding.

Like we were in this together.

I couldn't believe this was the man I'd had sex with a couple of days ago. I couldn't believe he could be so hot and masculine and also so... sweet.

By the end of the tea party, I was well on my way to swooning.

I couldn't swoon though. Not over Declan. This was too serious. I couldn't let Lily get too attached, and I definitely couldn't get too attached to him myself.

Declan wasn't—he just wasn't—the kind of guy to stick around.

He was the guy for one night. He wasn't the guy for forever.

"Mommy?" Lily said later on the drive home, pulling me out of my brooding reverie.

"What, honey?"

"Does Mr. Curtis like you?"

I was so surprised I actually jerked, barely managing not to jerk the steering wheel. "What? What are you talking about?"

She looked concerned at my tone, which was harsher than it should have been. "I was just wondering. He wants to be around you a lot."

I searched my mind, wondering what in our behavior had clued the girl in. I couldn't think of anything since all our more intimate encounters had been when she wasn't around. "We both work at the school, so we end up in the same place sometimes."

"He looks at you like he likes you."

I had no idea what to say to that.

"It's okay if he likes you, isn't it?" she added, an edge of concern in her voice.

"What do you mean?"

"Daddy is dead, so it's okay for you to have a boyfriend, right?"

For a minute, I was too stunned to speak. It rarely surprised me anymore when Lily said something that was so beyond her years, but this? This was more than I knew how to handle.

"Mommy?" she prompted.

"Right. It's okay. But Mr. Curtis isn't going to be my boyfriend." My mind was a confused whirl, and I just prayed I was handling this right. This was the first time the subject had ever come up.

"Why not?"

"Because we don't like each other that way."

"Maybe you do and you don't know it yet."

"I don't think so, sweetheart. But one day I might like someone that way." I met her eyes in the rearview mirror. "How would you feel about that?"

She reflected for a minute before she answered. "I would feel okay. We can still love Daddy, right?"

"Of course we can. We'll always love Daddy." For no good reason, I felt tears burn in my eyes.

It was so unfair—brutally unfair—that Nick had to miss out on all these years of being a father to Lily.

Lily nodded. "So it's okay if we want to love someone else."

I checked her expression and saw nothing but confidence. She believed it. She wasn't conflicted. In her mind, there was no problem with loving a father who was dead and loving another man too.

The knowledge eased something I hadn't known was anxious in my heart, but it generated a different sort of anxiety. "That's good. That's right. But Mr. Curtis isn't that man, Lily."

"Oh. Okay."

I checked the mirror, and she looked content, staring out at the park we were passing. I breathed a sigh of relief, glad we'd gotten through that hurdle unscathed.

We were almost at home when Lily said out of the blue, "I think it's a disting possibility."

I frowned. "*Distinct*, honey."

"Distinct," she repeated, pronouncing the word carefully. "I think it's a distinct possibility."

"What is?"

"That Mr. Curtis is the man."

I closed my eyes and groaned.

There was nothing I could say.

I didn't have any duties at lunch the next day, so I planned to make good use of the time, finishing the lesson plans I hadn't done the previous afternoon thanks to our impromptu tea party. Normally, getting behind on my work bothered me, but this time—since it was for something that meant so much to Lily—I didn't mind.

I'd brought a sandwich from home, so I just ran to the teacher's lounge for a cup of coffee before heading back to my classroom.

Declan seemed to come out of nowhere, falling in step with me in the hall. "Hello," he said with a smile that was almost intimate.

I blushed. Like an idiot. "Hello."

"How is your day going?"

"Okay. I'm trying to get some work done over lunch since I'm not on duty."

"Neither am I." There was a strange resonance to his tone—sexy, teasing, and naughty at the same time.

I took a deep breath and looked away from him. "You should try to get some work done too. Even if you're not a real teacher—" I'd been speaking softly, but I broke off at his quick look. "Even so, you're responsible for these kids' education."

"I know that. I've been killing myself trying to do a decent job while still watching out for Jessileigh. Believe me, it hasn't been a walk in the park."

I knew it hadn't. And honestly, I was surprised and appreciative that he'd done as well as he had. Even Lily wasn't complaining about his teaching anymore.

But I couldn't let the softness show since I definitely wasn't supposed to be feeling affectionate and admiring of him. "So you shouldn't waste time you could be using to prepare for class," I said rather primly. "There's always something to be done—papers to grade, lesson plans to review. And I'm quite certain you have work to do for the Christmas pageant."

He grinned at me, and his expression changed to one I recognized. "I love when you get all prim and talk like a teacher."

My cheeks grew hot, and I dropped my eyes. "I am a teacher."

He leaned in and murmured, "It makes me hot. That

was another one of my fantasies. The naughty school teacher."

He was making me hot too. I was all too aware of his expression, his body, the heat and tension I could feel vibrating off him.

"Have you thought any more about... possibilities?" he asked in that same thick tone.

I knew exactly what he was talking about. I nodded. "I've thought about it. As long as we keep it simple and no strings, then I guess we can—"

I broke off because I couldn't speak. He'd taken my arm and was dragging me with him. I had no idea where until we'd reached a supply closet. Before I knew it, we were inside.

"What are we doing?" I gasped when he closed the door and turned around with a hot look.

His hands slid from my shoulders down to my hips and pulled my pelvis toward him firmly. I groaned low in my throat when I felt the hard bulge of his erection against my middle.

"What do you think we're doing?" he murmured huskily, backing me up against a small table in the corner.

I felt my butt connect with the edge and shuddered as Declan pressed the entire length of his body up against me. "In a closet?" I whispered foolishly, feeling like I might melt away.

Declan heaved me up until I was propped on the edge of the table. "I told you it was one of my fantasies," he said thickly.

"We...we shouldn't..." I protested mildly, even as I clung to his shoulders while he started unbuttoning my blouse.

When he'd gotten enough of the buttons undone, he lowered his mouth and spoke over my bra. "Only convenient place at the moment." Then he gave me a sexy grin. "Funny how that worked out, right?"

The vibrations on my breast made me moan helplessly. But as I cupped the back of his head with my hands and held his face more firmly to my chest, I managed to say, "Not much for patience, are you?"

He sucked hard on my nipple through the fabric of my bra, causing me to gasp harshly. "I'm about as far from patient as possible." His tongue teased me. "I can't stop thinking about you. I'm frustrated as hell right now."

My head fell back when he started teasing my nipple once more with his tongue. "Maybe I am too."

I was grateful I'd worn a skirt when he started bunching it up around my hips. Then his hand found the damp spot in my panties, and he made a throaty sound of approval against my breast.

I gave a little gasp when he raised his head, adjusted my weight on the table, and then parted my legs. "You better have a condom."

"I do," he said, reaching into his back pocket. "I was hoping you'd change your mind sometime soon. Actually, I prayed that you would. Every minute of every day."

Feeling precarious and off-balance on the little table, I held on to his broad shoulders as he unfastened his pants.

I felt wild and a little naughty to be having sex like this, with most of our clothes on, in the closet in the middle of the day.

I reached down with one hand to stroke his freed erection, thrilled when he moaned under my light touch.

"Now," Declan grunted after a minute. "What was it you wanted?"

I parted my legs and tried to move him into position. "I thought you were the one who wanted it."

He rolled on the condom and clamped his hands down on my hips and angled them slightly. Then positioned himself at my entrance. "I'm pretty sure you want it too," he rasped, teasing me mercilessly with tiny, tantalizing thrusts.

Sucking in an urgent breath and clawing at his shoulders, I hissed. "Inside me, Declan. I want you inside me."

He drove his pelvis forward, fitting himself inside me in one swift thrust.

I swallowed a sound of pleasure as he filled me with perfect, delicious pressure. I adjusted my hips until I was more comfortable on the edge of the table and brought my legs up to hook around his thighs.

"You do want this, don't you?" he asked, his voice a hot breath against my ear.

"Yeah," I gasped, clenching around him possessively. "God, yeah."

On a hoarse grunt, he pulled back, pausing for a beat. Then he hooked one of his elbows under my knee, pulling me open more completely before he pushed back in—the momentum of his thrust forcing me back and up, only halted by his strong hands gripping me from behind. "Like that?" he gritted through his clenched jaw.

I bit my lip to keep from crying out, but my neck twitched erratically, tossing my head to the side. The delicious friction sent sharp sensations shooting out from my center. "Yeah. Just like that."

He withdrew and thrust again.

My arms had somehow gotten twined around his neck, and I leaned forward until my mouth was at his ear. "Hard," I whispered. "I need it hard, Declan."

I could hardly believe this was me.

Sweet little Kristin Andrews was suddenly behaving like a very naughty woman.

And I was beginning to like this side of me.

Especially with Declan.

He took me harder. My leg that was hanging over his arm bounced with our rhythm, and I felt the jolts of pleasure from each thrust start coalescing into a swell of rising pressure. He must have been feeling it too, because soon he couldn't maintain his steady rhythm.

Making little noises with the tempo of our motion, I pulled back to look at his face. I saw that his expression was twisted with effort and concentration, and I knew we didn't have very long.

Feeling stable now on the table in the strength of his arms, I eased one of my hands past my bunched up skirt down to where we were joined, rubbing myself to speed things up.

The pleasure immediately intensified, and my inner muscles instinctively clasped at his hard flesh.

His hot, wild gaze had followed my hand, and a primal sound burst out from his throat. Declan started grunting out rough monosyllables now, and I heard him pant, "Come, Kristin. Come."

I rocked frantically against him, trying to reach that peak.

"Come," he grunted, this time with rough authority.

So I did.

I hissed in pleasure and bit down over the fabric on his shoulder as I felt the familiar waves of pleasure overtake me. My fingernails raked over the skin on the back of his neck. My head falling backward, I saw Declan's face transform as he finally let himself come. My muscles clamped down around him as he kept pushing into me, muffling the sound of his own release against my neck.

My throat felt raw, and my breath was raspy as I started to relax. I clung to him tightly as the contractions faded. His body was hot and shaking a little under my arms, and his mouth on the skin of my throat was warm and moist.

He finally raised his damp face. Gazed at me for a long moment. Then kissed me gently, his tongue sweetly stroking my mouth.

When the kiss finally broke, I leaned against him, hot, breathless, and trembling. I couldn't believe we'd just done that.

I couldn't believe *I'd* just done that.

I'd never done something like that before in all my life.

His arms were still wrapped around me, but one of his hands now slid up until he was cupping my cheek, tilting my head back until I was meeting his eyes. "That was amazing," he murmured.

"Mm hmm." That was as articulate as I could be at the moment.

"*You* are amazing." He caressed my cheek with his thumb.

I swallowed hard at the wave of emotion that washed over me at the tender gesture and the look in his eyes, different but just as powerful as the physical sensations of before. "You're kind of okay yourself," I managed to say, hoping to lighten the mood.

His smile broadened. "Glad to hear it."

I was feeling so soft and emotional that I had to remind myself that this was just a fling. Sex and nothing else. "I had no idea that casual sex with no strings could be so hot," I said, pitching my tone as teasing.

He blinked and didn't answer for just a moment. Then he smiled again. "I think any sex between you and me is going to be hot. Strings or no strings."

"True." I really had to pull myself together since I was starting to read things into his words and expression. I pulled away from him physically as the first step. "Okay... well, uh...." Suddenly, I was at a loss for words. There was a part of me that wanted to lean in and linger, but I knew I couldn't.

Shouldn't.

So I pasted a smile on my face as I finished smoothing

my skirt. "That was fun, but I better get back. My lunch break is almost over."

"Mine too." He straightened his clothes and ran a hand over his face like he was still a little befuddled.

But there was no way he was as befuddled as me. It wasn't possible. "Talk to you later," I said quickly, and then I left with a wave of my hand.

I ran to the bathroom to bring my body and my mind into some sort of order.

But ever since Declan had entered my life, all order and reason seemed to have vanished.

10

DECLAN

It takes a lot to throw me.

And I was thrown.

It took a solid five minutes before I could even think of leaving the damn closet because I was completely out of my element here. I'd seduced dozens of women in my life, and I'd been seduced by just as many. But what just happened here with Kristin was far beyond anything I'd ever experienced.

And it scared the hell out of me.

You'd think I'd be happy, right? I mean, what man wouldn't be over the freaking moon to have a woman who was all prim and proper one minute and a total sex goddess the next?

Me, that's who.

I knew almost from the start that there was an attraction between us—hell, I pursued her with single-minded intent. I never wanted to get involved with a woman with a kid, and if anything, Lily was the perfect excuse to keep this simple. Uncomplicated. But now? I don't particularly feel like I want that anymore.

Quickies in a storage closet are all fine and good, but watching her walk out the door had felt... wrong. I wanted her here with me. I wanted to hold her, kiss her... have more time with her. And even though I knew she had to leave—after all, we couldn't stay in the supply closet all day—but there was still that element of her running from me that left me feeling a little sick inside.

Shit.

There was no way that I was *actually* feeling this way. It... it had to be something else. Maybe the fumes from the cleaning products in the closet were messing with my brain because I was so *not* the guy who was looking for anything more than a good time.

But who was I kidding. I couldn't keep lying to myself, and I couldn't keep having this same inner argument either. Something was changing, and it didn't matter how much I tried to fight it. It was happening.

I was just trying to figure out which argument I was fighting for.

I straightened my clothes and fumbled for the light switch just to get my bearings. No one was in the hallway when Kristin walked out, but I wasn't stupid enough to think we'd have that kind of luck twice. So I grabbed a box of tissues, some hand sanitizer and some paper towels, and carefully opened the door.

The coast was clear, and I all but ran back to my

classroom. Once there, I looked around the room and cursed. Kristin had a valid point earlier. I should have used my time to do some stuff for lesson planning or at least stayed close to the cafeteria to keep an eye on Jessileigh. After all, that was the reason for my even being here.

Not to have hot sex in a storage closet with a fellow teacher.

No matter how much she turned me on.

I dropped my unnecessary supplies on my desk and made my way back to the cafeteria. I needed to remember why I was here. I needed to focus on doing the job I was hired to do. Maybe if I could keep my thoughts out of my pants and get my head on straight, things would be a lot less complicated. I needed to be on alert at all times. Just because Jessileigh's mom was playing nice right now didn't mean she was going to continue on that path. And there was no way I'd be able to live with myself if something happened to that little girl while I was off being a screw-up.

Hadn't I learned that lesson already? Didn't I know better?

The sad truth was that I had learned it, but there was something about Kristin that was... different. I didn't feel like I was being a screw-up when I was with her. I didn't feel like our time together was just casual or for fun. Being with her made me want to be a better person, a better man.

Now I just had to find a way to balance it all out and

see if she was interested in maybe a little something more than this casual thing.

"No. Absolutely not. You need to stop this right now. I'm not kidding."

I was driving through town on my way to my hotel after school and decided that I needed to talk to someone. Levi was busy. Sebastian was unavailable.

That was how I ended up with Cole.

"I think you're overreacting a bit, man," I said with a nervous chuckle. "Seriously. Relax."

"Hell no!" he snapped back. "What is it with you guys? Why the hell can't you just be happy with the way things were… are? I mean, we've been over this before, and I'm seriously considering getting a fucking tape recorder and just hitting the play button because it's getting annoying to have to keep repeating myself."

He'd lost me. But that was nothing new. Cole had a tendency to ramble on about stuff that none of us remembered. "Refresh my memory. What exactly have you been repeating?"

Cole growled into the phone. "Okay, first it was Levi. I was willing to let that one slide because it's Harper. They'd known each other for most of their lives, and it was bound to happen. Sebastian? That was just crazy. I know he sort of got thrown together with Ali because he was keeping an eye on her with that case and all that crap, but still. He didn't have to go and ask her to marry him. And now you."

"Hey... Whoa. I'm not asking Kristin to marry me," I said defensively.

"Not yet. But I can tell. I can just fucking tell that it's not going to be long."

"You're wrong," I mumbled and cursed under my breath. "Look, all I'm saying is that... I just want to spend some time with her."

"And the kid."

I nodded. "And Lily. They're a package deal. I'm just not sure how to interact with kids."

"Says the first grade teacher," Cole said with a snicker.

"Grow up. I am the first to admit that I wasn't the right one for this job, but I was the only one available. I didn't like it at first, but I'm dealing with it. It's not like I have a choice. So I'm here, and no one's been scarred for life."

"We don't know that for sure."

I wanted to argue, but he kind of had a point. "I may not be winning any teacher-of-the-year awards, but I've certainly gotten better. I'm following the lesson plan thing about seventy percent of the time, and the principal is making sure that I'm not skipping anything vital. All in all, I'd say that the kids are all right."

Cole made a noncommittal sound. "If you say so. But that's not the point. We were talking about you and hot teacher."

"Kristin. Her name is Kristin." My teeth were clenched,

and I didn't want to think about the hot flash of rage I felt at anyone talking about Kristin in a derogatory way.

"Okay, whatever. You and *Kristin*." He sighed dramatically. "What's the holdup then? You want to hang out with her, clearly she's into you, so what's the problem?"

"She wants casual. She wants a fling—no strings, no commitments. We agreed to that. She hasn't really been involved with anyone since her husband died, and she sort of sees me as a safe way to have some fun without it getting too serious."

"Why does she think that?"

"Seriously? Look at me. I'm the poster boy for having a good time with no strings attached."

"Okay, wow. Thinking a little highly of yourself there, aren't you?"

"I didn't mean it like it's a good thing," I said, feeling more than a little exhausted with this conversation. Why couldn't Levi or Seb been available? "Let's just say that I'm not the white-picket-fence type of guy. I never wanted to be. Having fun, flirting? That's me."

"Obviously it's not anymore, or we wouldn't be having this fucking stupid conversation."

That was it. Cole didn't understand. Hell, I'm not even sure that I understood what I was feeling. "You know what? Forget that I called. It's nothing. I'll handle it."

"All right, all right. Get your panties out of their knot."

"They're not…"

"So you admit that you wear panties," Cole said and then burst out laughing.

It was hard not to join in. "I can't wait until you hit puberty," I said after a minute. "You're an ass."

"Yeah, but right now I'm the only ass available to talk you down from the ledge."

"I'm not on the ledge." *Much.* "I just needed to bounce these thoughts off someone. I don't know what to do. I don't know how much longer I'm going to be on this case or how much time I have with Kristin. I'm afraid that I'm going to come on too strong and scare her off or that I'll do something stupid with the kid and ruin everything."

"It seems to me like you've bonded with the kid. From everything you've told me, Lily has your back."

I couldn't help but smile. Lily had actually been a lifesaver in the classroom. Not just with Jessileigh, but with me too. Whenever I was struggling with keeping things on task or trying to remember where we were supposed to be and when, Lily was there to offer her two cents and her input. I resented it at first, and then I realized what an asset she was.

Besides being a great kid.

"She does," I finally said. "But... it's a big responsibility —you know, it's not like I'd just be dating Kristin. If things didn't work out, I'd have invested time in a relationship with Lily too. The kid's already lost her father. I'm not sure how she'd react to having another man disappear from her life."

"Shit. I hadn't really thought of it like that." He paused. "And tell me again why you can't just keep it casual with the mom?"

"Because I don't want to. I'm not digging the sneaking around while Lily's with her grandparents or sex in a supply closet thing anymore. Actually, I'm feeling a bit... used."

A hearty laugh escaped from Cole's mouth, and I wanted to strangle him. "Dude, you did *not* just say that! You're feeling used? You?"

"Can you just be serious? For a fucking minute?" I yelled. "Damn it! I'm really struggling here, and you laughing at me isn't helping at all!"

Cole instantly sobered. "Okay, you want help? Here it is. You're moving pretty fast here. You're not used to *not* being in control in a relationship. Even in your most casual of hookups, you called the shots. It seems to me like you're spending a lot of time waiting on Kristin and taking your cues from her. And unfortunately, that's what you're going to have to continue to do. You don't want to mess up her life or Lily's. If you want to know where you stand? You're going to have to talk to her. Instead of getting naked with her next time, talk to her. Get to know her a little more and feel her out—not up." He chuckled. "Sorry. Last time, I promise."

I sighed. "You're right. This is foreign territory to me, and I guess I'm not used to having to be patient—or take my cue from anyone else. I just wish it wasn't so... complicated."

"Well, it is. And it may stay like that for a long time. If you're really serious about this, you're going to have to learn to be patient. Just talk to her. Make the time to actually talk to her so maybe she doesn't feel like she's just a fling or booty call to you."

"Okay, can you stop saying booty call? It just sounds... wrong."

Cole chuckled. "You are so screwed."

I gave a mirthless laugh. "Yeah. I know."

The next two days at school were hectic. We had to spend a lot more time working on the Christmas pageant, and thankfully, Chuck took pity on me and had one of the music teacher assistants come and work with my class instead of me doing it. Don't get me wrong, I still had to be there and do some stuff on my own with the kids, but the majority of the preparations were done by the music teacher.

Dodged that bullet.

I hardly saw Kristin. She seemed a little more distracted than usual, and whenever I got within a few feet of her, there was always someone close by who needed her attention.

I needed her attention, dammit.

Lily must have noticed because she came up to me with a big smile on her face. "What's up, Lil?" I asked. I probably shouldn't have been so informal with her, but it just slipped out.

"You're smiling at my mom," she said, almost singing the statement.

"What? No. No, I'm not." Maybe I was being a little defensive.

"It's okay," she said lightly as she started to hop from one foot to the other. If anything, her smile seemed to grow. "She smiles when she watches you too."

"Really?" And now I sounded a little too hopeful.

She nodded. "Uh-huh."

So many questions began to form in my mind.

"I like seeing her smile. It makes me happy," Lily said, still hopping.

"What do you..." But the kid had skipped off. Was I desperate enough that I was going to ask a six-year-old for relationship advice?

Maybe.

By the time I looked back across the room, Kristin and her class were walking out of the auditorium. She looked back, and our eyes met, and all I wanted to do was walk over to her and kiss her and just ask how her day was going.

To quote Cole, I was so screwed.

I had the kids lined up at the end of the day like I always did, with Jess and me at the back of the line. The first bell rang, and my little bus riders walked out of the room, playing follow the leader out and down the hall. We waited quietly for the second bell for the carpool kids.

I felt uneasy. It wasn't something I could pinpoint and

put my finger on, but it was like that sixth sense you get when you know something's going to happen. The last time I remember feeling that way was that fateful day in the dessert.

The day we lost Gavin.

I had been distracted by the feeling, but I wasn't going to let that happen today. Reaching down, I took Jessileigh's hand in mine. She looked up at me, her eyes huge, and it was as if she sensed something too. Doing my best to relax and reassure her that everything was fine, I smiled. "Any plans for after school today, Jess?" I asked.

She had finally relaxed with me calling her that. "Daddy said that we were going to go horseback riding if it wasn't too cold."

I chuckled. The kid was bundled up in a hat, coat, scarf, and mittens. Chances were there wasn't going to be riding of any kind today. "And what if it is too cold? What's the plan after that?"

She shrugged. "Hot chocolate and coloring."

"That sounds like a great way to spend the afternoon, if you ask me," I said.

"Really? You like coloring?"

I nodded my head. "And hot chocolate. It's one of my favorite winter drinks." I couldn't help but keep grinning at the look on her face. She seemed very pleased by my response. "I especially like it with the little marshmallows."

"Me too!" she exclaimed, her entire face lighting up.

"Well, that's because you're very smart," I said.

"Mr. Curtis?" she asked shyly.

"Yeah?"

"Do you... do you think that maybe we can have hot chocolate at our Christmas party?"

It wasn't quite the question I was expecting. "Of course. I'm sure we can ask one of the moms to make it for us." Then I noticed that some of the brightness left her angelic face. "What? What's the matter, Jess?"

She shook her head at first, but I crouched down beside her until she looked at me. "Sometimes... sometimes I wish that my mom was like the other moms."

I felt like I had been kicked in the gut, and I could have kicked myself to bringing up the subject. The kid didn't often talk about her family stuff—particularly her mom—but it was clear that it bothered her. "You know, not all moms are alike," I began diplomatically. "Some moms are great at baking while others don't even know how. My mom used to make the best spaghetti and meatballs, but she always burned the cookies."

"Really?" she asked, her eyes going wide again.

I nodded. "Really."

"But... did she come to your Christmas pageants?"

I shook my head. "We didn't really have those when I was in school. My mom worked a lot when I was your age, and so she didn't always get to come to my school stuff. My dad came even less."

"My daddy always comes to school stuff," she said, sounding a bit more confident. "And he even has tea parties with me at home."

An image of my tea party with Lily and Kristin instantly sprang to mind, but I pushed it aside to focus on this important conversation.

"That's because he's a good dad and he loves you."

She smiled. "I think you're a good dad, Mr. Curtis."

"Me? Oh, Jess," I said with a nervous laugh. "I'm not a dad."

"Lily says that you like her mom and that maybe you would be her dad. I told her that she was lucky. She told me that her real dad died and she was sad. If you became her dad, then she'd have two. One in heaven and one here." Big blue eyes blinked up at me like this was the most normal conversation in the world.

I thought I was going to be sick. I stood back up and felt a cold sweat begin to cover my entire body as my heart fought to make its way out of my chest. I had no idea how long I stood there until Jess tugged on my hand. "The bell rang. We have to go."

"Oh... right." I felt like I was having an out-of-body experience. We walked down the long hall toward the front entrance of the school, and yet I felt like I was watching myself do it. Once outside, the cold wind whipped around me.

"There's Lily! Hi, Lily! I'll see you tomorrow!" Jessileigh called as she walked with me toward the spot where they usually waited. I didn't even turn my head to see why Lily was outside. Usually she and Kristin didn't leave until after all the carpool kids were gone. Then I remembered that it was probably Kristin's day to have carpool duty.

I scanned the area in search of Mr. Vanderhall's car. We had talked on the phone last night, and he had mentioned that he was getting worried—Mitzi had been quiet for too long. He had a feeling that with Christmas approaching that she'd try something. I was in total agreement with him on that front. We talked strategy for him and his home security team, and I offered to be around over the holidays if they needed me.

It wasn't as if I had any plans.

"There's my dad!" Jess called out and pulled her hand from mine.

"Jess! Wait!" I called as she ran forward. It wasn't like her to take off like that without me. She knew the drill. We always walked to the car together.

It all happened so fast. One minute I had a clear view of her. The next she was gone. There were screeching tires, and when I saw her again, I saw that it wasn't Mr. Vanderhall's car at all. It looked just like it, and that certainly wasn't her father in the driver's seat. With nothing more than a quick glance, I was positive that it was Mitzi Vanderhall driving.

"Jess! Stop!" I ran through the small crowd of students and teachers—my only thought was to get to Jessileigh before she got into the wrong car or got hurt. I called her name again, and she finally stopped and turned, but she was already in the middle of the driveway.

The car that she thought was hers swerved around the cars in front of it and sped dangerously fast toward us. I had to act quickly.

Grabbing her, I was about to turn toward the sidewalk. I could hear the car getting closer.

"Declan? What's—" It was Kristin.

"Take her!" I said and shoved Jessileigh in her direction. "*Now!*"

The last thing I saw was Kristin's arms around Jessileigh as she pulled her back.

The last thing I felt was a car slamming into me before everything went black.

11

KRISTIN

IN MOVIES, PEOPLE ALWAYS SCREAM IMMEDIATELY WHEN THEY see something horrifying happen. It's supposed to be the natural reaction. Not for me though. My throat closes. My eyes blur over. I freeze, unable to think, unable to move, unable to make a sound.

That was exactly what I did when I saw Declan get hit by the car. I was watching, so I saw the whole thing unfold in slow motion. He pushed Jessileigh toward me, and I grabbed her in my arms, holding her tight. The approaching car didn't stop, and Declan couldn't get out of the way.

I saw his body jerk at the impact. I heard the squeal of brakes. I saw him get thrown off his feet to land in an awkward heap on the pavement.

Then other people were screaming. Children and a couple of teachers and other parents. And a lot of things were happening all at once. People running forward. The car that had just hit Declan backing up with a violent lurch, scraping the front of another car that was unfortunately close.

Someone was on the phone, calling 911, I assumed. And several people leaned down over where Declan was prone on the ground.

I was a teacher, an authority figure. I should be cool and composed and help everyone else get through this crisis situation.

Plus I knew Declan better than anyone else here.

But I was frozen, my arms still tightly around Jessileigh. Shielding her from the horror unfolding in front of us. And I could do... nothing.

There was a black tidal wave of fear and pain that I was barely holding at bay. If I moved, it might unleash.

"He's alive," I heard someone say. I think it was the mother of one of the students. She was a veterinarian, which was probably as close to a doctor as we had available at the moment. "He got knocked out, but he's breathing, and his vitals feel strong."

I could suddenly breathe, letting out an exhale in a whoosh. I loosened my arms around Jessileigh, who was crying.

A murmur of relief had followed this announcement, and Jessileigh turned to me through her tears and asked, "Is Mr. Curtis okay?"

"I hope so," I said, finding my voice again. I took a few ragged breaths. "He's hurt, but I think he'll be okay."

I had no reason to believe this, other than hopeful

thinking and the fact that he hadn't died on impact. But I had to say something, and I was praying it was true.

I heard a familiar whimper and turned around to see Lily running over toward me. I reached out my arm to hug her against me, feeling more myself, able to function again—although I was still shaky and terrified.

And that black tidal wave was still hovering over me, ready to descend at any minute.

I knew far too well how quickly disaster could strike, how tenuous any peace and security really was. When Nick had died, it was with a sudden, devastating blow. No warning. No preparation. Just love ripped out of your life with a violent force.

It wasn't something that could be lived through twice.

"Is he going to die like Daddy?" Lily whispered, her little hands clinging to my sweater.

I almost choked on the question, on what it implied. "I don't think so, sweetie. He's just gotten knocked out. It happens when someone gets hit on the head too hard."

Lily nodded and looked over at Jessileigh, who was wiping her eyes with her fists. "Are you okay, Jessileigh?" Lily asked.

The other girl nodded as tears streamed down her face. "Mr. Curtis saved me."

It was true. I had seen it happen. The car must have been driven by the girl's mother, who was making a desperate ill-advised attempt to snatch her. She'd already screeched out of the parking lot, but maybe the cops would get her now.

Another murmur in the crowd began, starting from those leaning over Declan. "He's awake," someone said.

I let out another loud exhale at his news. Maybe he wasn't hurt too much. Maybe he would be okay.

Maybe it was irrational since I hadn't really known him for that long. But I didn't want to think about the world without Declan in it.

"Kristin," someone called. One of the teachers who was kneeling down next to the veterinarian. "He's asking for you."

I swallowed hard and looked for someone to stay with the girls before I would even consider moving. Luckily, Chuck was right there and seemed to know what I was thinking. "Go ahead," he murmured. "I've got them." We shared a look of understanding before I forced myself to loosen my grip on them.

With a shaky breath, I stumbled over, lowering myself in the space they made for me. My heart was racing, and I felt vaguely sick at how pale Declan looked and at the blood running from his temple to his cheekbone and already matting in his hair.

His eyes were half-opened though, and they landed on me. "Jess?" he asked in barely a croak.

"She's fine. I had her." Swallowing hard, I added, "She's safe."

This was evidently a relief to him, and I felt a strange wave of affection at how much he was committed to keeping safe whomever was under his care.

Then his expression changed, and his eyes warmed

with a look that was unmistakably soft and fond. He was gazing at me that way. "Don't be scared," he mumbled, shifting his position in a way that obviously gave him great pain.

He knew me too well.

"I'm fine," I lied. I was terrified.

He seemed to realize this because his look softened even more. "And don't... don't... let them shave off my... hair."

A few hours later, I was in a hospital room with him.

I'm not exactly sure how it happened, really.

The police and ambulance came. They took Declan away, but I had to stay and answer a lot of questions with the others who had seen the incident.

I made sure the Jessileigh was safely with her father—thanks to Chuck's help and confirmation. My head was spinning with all that was going on around me. Then Lily's grandparents took Lily home with them since everyone seemed to think I'd want to get right to the hospital to be with Declan.

I don't know why everyone assumed that since we certainly weren't a couple. As far as anyone knew, we were simply co-workers.

Co-workers who slept together, but no one else knew about that. But still, everyone acted sweet and concerned with me as if Declan was an important person in my life.

He wasn't supposed to be.

But there was still that dark tidal wave, waiting to crash over me, drown me. And that shouldn't be there if Declan was really just a fling.

I went to the hospital though. I had to know that he was okay. They'd already given him a room, and the nurse told me that since he had a concussion, he was allowed to doze off for a few minutes but he shouldn't be allowed to sleep long. He would have to stay the night just to make sure he was okay. He had a couple of cracked ribs, but otherwise it was just the damage to his head.

His eyes were closed when I entered the room, so I moved carefully, walking over to the chair next to the bed.

They'd shaved a little of his hair, around where the bandage was. He looked paler than normal and strangely young with his eyes closed.

He looked vulnerable. Breakable. Human.

He could die. He almost had.

The thought hurt so much I raised a hand to my chest, trying to pull myself together. I hadn't quite done it when his eyes suddenly opened.

"Hey, beautiful."

It amazed me how even in this condition, he was able to come off like he was flirting. It made me smile.

And then it made me want to cry because he looked so...broken.

"I'm okay, Kristin," he said softly. His voice was still hoarse, but it wasn't nearly as broken as it had been before the ambulance had arrived.

"I know." I took a shaky breath, telling myself for the hundredth time that my reaction was absolutely ridiculous.

Declan wasn't dead.

He was here and he was alive and breathing.

He'd saved a little girl's life.

I swallowed hard because it wasn't just that—it wasn't just the accident or what he'd done that was threatening to overwhelm me. It was how much I was feeling for him. And not just right now, but all the time.

I had to push those feelings aside.

We were just supposed to be casual.

And we weren't a couple.

He reached out toward me, and recognizing what he wanted, I adjusted my arm so he could take my hand. "It's just a concussion."

"And broken ribs."

"I've had broken ribs before. They hurt like hell but aren't the end of the world."

I nodded, feeling emotion tightening in my throat again.

His expression went a little serious. "Where's Lily?" he asked, glancing over toward the door before his eyes returned to my face. He was quieter than normal, without his typical charm. I kind of liked it. It felt more real.

But it was also incredibly unsettling.

"With Nick's parents. She was upset and wanted to come see you, but I didn't think it was a good idea until I knew what was happening."

He nodded. "Tell her she can come visit me later on." His hand shifted until he was stroking my palm with his thumb. "I'm glad you came though."

My breath caught in my throat. "Yeah."

He was looking at me deeply, with an intensity I wasn't used to. As if he was telling me something with his eyes.

Something I desperately wanted to hear.

And something that caused a rising panic to run through me.

"Kristin," he murmured.

"Yeah." My response was brief, a little wobbly. I was holding my breath.

"Is this still a fling?"

"I... I don't know."

His lips turned up in a little smile as if he was pleased by my response. I don't know why—since I didn't even know what my response meant.

"Come here," he said.

"What?"

He lifted a hand toward me. "I can't move much with these damned ribs, so you have to come here."

I moved closer, so rattled I was pretty much clueless.

He smiled, his full, warm smile. "You need to lean down farther." When I just stared in confusion, he added, "Damn it, I want to kiss you, and I can't reach."

I gave a surprised giggle and leaned down so he could take my head in his hand. Then he lifted his enough to press his mouth against mine.

A shiver of excitement and pleasure and feeling ran

through me. I kissed him back, our lips gently brushing against each other.

"That's better," he murmured against my mouth.

Smiling, I kissed him again.

I was pretty much completely overwhelmed when a voice from behind me said, "Oops. Bad timing."

I jerked back and straightened up, my cheeks blazing with embarrassment. When I turned around, I saw two men I'd never seen before, standing in the doorway.

They were both well built and handsome, and they both looked like they could handle themselves really well in a fight. I instinctively knew these must be men who worked with Declan.

"Very bad timing," Declan said, but he was smiling as he waved them in. "What are you guys doing here?"

"We heard you took a little tumble, so we figured we better hurry down to hold your hand." The man who was slightly taller and who looked a little less rough smiled at me. "But I see you already have that covered."

Declan gave his friend a good-natured snarl. "Kristin, these are two of my partners in the company. The smart-ass is Levi, and the silent, glowering one is Cole."

I shook hands with both men in turn, still feeling flustered and strangely self-conscious. These men were studying me with a kind of amused interest, as if they were both pleased and surprised by my presence.

"Where's Seb?"

"He couldn't get away," Levi said. "But he said to let him know if you were still breathing."

Declan laughed and then winced when it evidently hurt his ribs.

I could tell his friends had been genuinely concerned and were relieved that he was okay. I could tell that this was the way they interacted with each other, using humor to express affection. But it still made me a little sick to hear the joke about Declan almost dying.

Nick had died. And there wasn't anything funny about that.

Suddenly I stood up. "I better get back to Lily," I said, trying to sound natural. "I'm glad you're okay."

"Thanks." He met my eyes, and there was that expression again. The soft, purposeful, serious one—as if something important was happening. "Bring her by to see me later this evening if you can."

"Okay." I suddenly needed to get out of here. Right now. Before I collapsed into an emotional puddle. "It was nice to meet you guys."

"You too," Cole said while Levi gave a friendly wave.

I was trembling when I got into the car, and it was a long time before the trembling stopped.

After an early supper with her grandparents, I took Lily to the hospital.

She wouldn't have stopped nagging me if I didn't, and I thought it was probably better for her to go so she could see for herself that Declan was okay.

I was ridiculously nervous as we got out of the car, though, and even more nervous when we took the elevator up and walked down the hall.

His friends weren't in the room when we peeked in, and Declan appeared to be asleep.

"Is he sleeping, Mommy?" Lily asked in a stage whisper that echoed all the way down the hall.

Declan turned his head and smiled when he saw us. It was his normal smile. Warm. Heart-stopping. "If I was, I'd be awake now. Come on in, Lily. I'm glad you came."

Lily's face broke into a wide grin, and she hurried over to the bed. "Are you feeling okay, Mr. Curtis? Mommy said your head and your ribs were banged up a little."

"They are. But I'm feeling a lot better already." Declan's eyes shifted up to my face for just a minute—his expression almost hungry—before he returned them to rest on Lily's face.

"I'm glad you're okay. You were very brave."

"Do you think so?"

"Yes, sir. You saved Jessileigh. Everyone says so."

"Everyone, huh?" He gave a huff of amusement. "I was just doing my job."

"You're a better teacher than I thought," Lily admitted soberly. "I'm sorry I thought you weren't any good."

He laughed louder this time. "Well, I'm not the best teacher in the world, but I'm glad I got the chance to get to know you."

"Me too." Lily nodded and then looked up at my face. "Mommy is too."

I gave a little, startled gasp at this sentiment, but Declan met my eyes. "I hope she is."

I felt another wave of panic, that black tidal wave getting a little closer. I cleared my throat. "Lily, what did you do with your picture for Mr. Curtis?"

She pulled a folded piece of construction paper out of her pocket. It was hopelessly wrinkled. "It's here. But can I go to the bathroom first?"

"Can't you hold it?" I asked. I suddenly wanted to get out of this room just as soon as possible before something happened that might crush me.

"I don't think so. I'm sorry, Mommy."

"That's okay. You can use Mr. Curtis's bathroom. Let me just check to make sure it's okay."

I walked into the connecting bathroom, and it looked clean and unused, so I helped her with the light and then closed the door.

I returned to the chair next to the bed, feeling anxious and shaky.

"What's wrong, Kristin?" Declan asked, reaching out for my hand again.

I let him take it because I loved how it felt, no matter how scared it made me. "What do you mean?"

"You know exactly what I mean." His voice was soft so Lily couldn't hear in the bathroom. "What are you so worried about?"

I shook my head and started to give a quick dismissal, but I stopped myself. He deserved the truth, so I needed to tell him. "I don't know. Today was intense. It was scary and overwhelming and... I don't know. It's just that everything feels so different now and..."

He was stroking my hand again, maybe because it was the only part of me he could touch. "Everything is different. I think we both know that, Kristin. Neither of us planned this, but you have to know that this isn't just a casual hook-up."

The sound of his low, husky voice washed over me, caressing something inside me but at the same time sounding off warning bells.

And the warning bells were too loud to ignore.

I inhaled with a raspy sound. "I know. But I don't think I can... I don't know if..."

His brows drew together, and for the first time he looked genuinely worried. "What do you mean? You can't tell me you don't feel for me the way I feel for you. We're in this together."

"I know." I turned away. "But today I was... terrified. If anything happened to you..." The emotions were so strong that I took a minute to compose myself before I continued. "I lost a man once. I can't live through it again. And with your job... It's just too much of a risk."

I wasn't even sure I was making sense, but evidently Declan understood me. His whole body froze tensely, and I saw a flash of something pained in his eyes for just a moment. "I can understand how you'd be afraid, but I'm fine. I'm *fine*. And how can you turn your back on something that could be so good, just out of fear?"

I almost choked. I had to clear my throat. "Sometimes

fear is the strongest thing. Sometimes it just is. I'm so sorry, but I can't. I can't even try." The look on his face was almost enough for me to reconsider, but I knew I couldn't. "I can't live through that again. And I can't do that to my daughter. Lily doesn't deserve that."

I was on the edge of tears, but I held myself together because I heard the toilet flush from the bathroom.

"Wash your hands," I called out.

"I am." Lily sounded faintly offended.

I turned back to Declan, and now he looked stiff, closed up, as if he'd put up his walls of protection. "You're wrong, Kristin. What we have is worth fighting for. Saying no to it is wrong."

"Maybe." My voice broke even as I said it. "But it's the only thing I can say."

Lily came out then, ending the conversation. And I was desperately relieved because it meant we could go. Leave. And getting out of this room was now the most important thing in the world.

I'd hurt Declan. Really bad. I couldn't stand it.

And I'd hurt myself too.

But the only other option would be to live with that black tidal wave of grief and catastrophe just waiting to strike. I knew I'd only be able to keep it at bay for so long.

And that would be so much worse.

"Give Mr. Curtis your picture, sweetie, and then we have to go."

"Already?"

"I'm sorry, but Mr. Curtis needs his rest."

Declan didn't say anything, but he watched as Lily carefully unfold the wrinkled paper. She straightened it out before she laid it on his stomach.

He stared down at the childish picture.

"This is our class," Lily explained when he didn't say anything. She was so sweet and earnest I felt my eyes burning. "This is you. And this is Mommy in the doorway. And this is our Christmas tree. And you see on the chalkboard it says, 'We are glad you are our teacher, Mr. Curtis.'"

I saw suppressed emotion shuddering on Declan's face as he gazed down, and his hand was just slightly shaky as he picked the drawing up. "Thank... you," he managed to say. "It's perfect."

Lily's face relaxed in relief. "I'm glad. I worked on it all afternoon. It's the best picture I've ever done, and I wanted to give it to you."

It was too much— I was about to crumple, and I couldn't stand to look any longer at the emotion reined in on Declan's face.

Or the hope on Lily's.

"Okay, Lily. That was really sweet to give it to him. Now let's let Mr. Curtis rest."

"Can I see him tomorrow?"

There was no way in hell I was going to take her for another visit. I was going to have to do a lot of explaining.

But it couldn't be now. Not when my whole world was falling apart.

"We'll see. Say goodbye."

Lily grabbed Declan's hand and shook it, evidently

thinking this was the most appropriate gesture of farewell at her disposal. Then I took her hand as we walked for the door.

I glanced back at Declan one last time over my shoulder. He was watching me go.

"I'm sorry," I mouthed, as if that would help at all.

And that was it. Lily and I walked out the door.

To a future that was safe and secure.

And utterly devastating.

12

DECLAN

I NEVER KNEW THAT SOMETHING COULD HURT SO DAMN much. Not my injuries from the accident—those were fairly minor—but watching Kristin and Lily walk out the door.

And not come back.

I kept thinking I was dreaming. Or at least in some pain-medication-induced haze.

But I wasn't.

Kristin had walked out of my life and took everything —all of my hope, all of my dreams—with her.

A week later and it was still with me. And it still hurt.

I was released from the hospital the next day. Levi had come and picked me up since I wasn't allowed to drive. At first I wanted to be pissed, but then I realized I also didn't have my car with me since I had arrived at the hospital in an ambulance.

"A thank you wouldn't kill you," he said to me once we were in his car and leaving the hospital.

I knew what he was doing—he was trying to distract me because he knew I was tense and on edge. Maybe he didn't know the exact reason for the way I was feeling, but he could sense it just the same.

"Thanks."

We drove to my hotel in silence. Once we were in my room, he went for the small-talk approach.

"Cole and I took care of getting your car yesterday. I wasn't sure if you saw it in the parking lot."

I hadn't, but I thanked him anyway.

I walked around the room, unsure of what to do with myself. I couldn't drive, my whole body hurt like hell, and all I wanted to do was be at school and see my kids.

And Kristin.

"Do you want to talk about it?" Levi asked after a solid five minutes of silence.

"Not much to say."

He sighed. "There's no way you could have known that Mrs. Vanderhall would pull a stunt like that. It shows how unstable she is. The cops had no trouble finding her and charging her with attempted kidnapping, assault with a motor vehicle, leaving the scene of an accident. Trust me, she's not going to be an issue anymore. You did a great job, Dec."

I looked at him as if he were crazy. "You think I'm upset over that?"

Now it was Levi's turn to look confused. "Aren't you?"

And then I realized it was safer to just agree with him. Nodding, I said, "I did what I had to do. I just hate that it had to go down that way. Jess is gonna be traumatized for a long time over this."

"It could have been much worse. You realize that, right? If you hadn't gotten to her first and her mother had? The scarring would have been way worse."

"Yeah." It still didn't make me feel any better about that particular situation. I did my job and I kept my client safe and we got the outcome we all wanted.

Well, where the case was concerned anyway.

Carefully raking a hand through my hair, I walked over to the wall of windows and just stared out at the town.

"This isn't about the case, is it?" Levi finally asked. He came to stand beside me. "What's going on?"

For weeks he'd been the one I most wanted to talk to and yet our schedules never seemed to mesh and I ended up talking with Cole. Now here I was with his undivided attention, and I had no idea what to say.

"Is it Kristin?"

"Yeah."

And still I didn't know what to say beyond that.

Levi turned and walked over to the sofa and sat down. "Do you know how much Harper hated me when we first came back?"

Looking at him, I shook my head.

"She was hurting and pissed off that I was there and Gavin wasn't. Hell, every time she looked at me, I was a reminder of that."

My head was starting to pound, and my legs hurt, and I decided that maybe sitting down wasn't a bad thing either. With a weary sigh, I joined him.

"It didn't matter what I was doing," he went on. "I could have brought her a basket of puppies, and she still would have looked at me with that hostile glare. It just about killed me every time."

"Obviously she got over it," I murmured. The mere fact that they were married now told me she had.

Levi chuckled. "Yeah but it didn't happen over night. I had to hold my ground and prove to her that I was someone she could trust and how I was just as devastated as she was that Gavin wasn't here."

"It's not the same thing, Levi. Kristin isn't upset because I'm here and her husband isn't." At least, I hoped that wasn't part of this. "She lost Nick in an accident. He was a SEAL but he wasn't killed in combat. It really was an accident. Seeing what happened yesterday... it freaked her out. Knowing that the work I do will put me in danger. She can't deal with it."

Levi was silent for a minute before asking, "Can you?"

"Can I what?"

"Can you honestly handle asking her to deal with that? Asking her to learn to be okay with the possibility of you getting hurt?"

I wanted to argue that I wouldn't get hurt again or how if I did it wouldn't be anything that we couldn't handle.

Then I remembered the look on Kristin's face as she left yesterday.

And then I wasn't so sure of anything anymore.

I went to the school and met with Chuck the next day. Another substitute—a real one—was brought in to take over my class. I know it sounds crazy, but I was kind of upset about that. Those kids had really gotten to me, and I hated the fact that someone else was in there, someone else was going to make sure they learned all their lines for the Christmas pageant.

Christ, I was losing it.

He assured me that I hadn't done any permanent damage to the kids and that they'd easily catch up on anything that I might have missed—or skipped—curriculum-wise. That did little to make me feel better. I already knew that Jessileigh wasn't in class that day, so there was no real reason for me to be there. Her father had kept her home due to the events of the previous day. Smart man.

I wanted to go down the hall and tell the kids goodbye. I wanted to thank them all for being patient with me and for being really good even when I didn't know what the hell I was doing. And I wanted to see Lily.

After that I wanted to head farther down the hall to see Kristin.

In the end, I didn't do either of those things. I shook Chuck's hand and thanked him for his help and left.

"Oh, Mr. Curtis," Rose said as I was walking out of the

office. "Are you okay? That was so brave what you did yesterday! We all just couldn't believe it!"

She was talking a mile a minute, and she looked flustered, but I also knew that she was genuinely concerned, and that made me smile. "I'm fine, Rose. Thanks."

"Should you even be out of the hospital so soon?"

I nodded. "Just a couple of broken ribs and a concussion. I've had them both before, so I know to be careful."

She stood there in front of me, her hands clasped and smiled. "Will you be coming back to teach?"

Shit. Chuck hadn't ratted me out to anyone, so no one knew that I wasn't really a teacher. I shook my head. "No. No, I won't be back." And damn if that didn't choke me up. Before I did something embarrassing—like cry—I leaned in and kissed Rose on the cheek. "Take care of yourself," I said. And walked out.

Out in the hallway, I stopped. It was literally like I was at a crossroad. If I turned to the left, I was heading down to the classrooms—toward Lily. And Kristin. If I turned around, I could go back into the office and ask Chuck about staying on until Christmas break. But if I turned right, I'd be outside. Away from the school. Away from the kids.

Away from Kristin.

The metal door slammed behind me as I stepped out into the sunlight. But it didn't warm me. I felt cold. Empty.

This is the way it had to be.

"I bet you're glad to be out of there," Sebastian said that night at dinner. The guys had all converged on me to make sure I was doing all right—healing and whatnot—and to close out the case. "I would've paid good money to see you teaching a room full of six-year-olds!"

"Yeah, yeah, yeah. Laugh it up. It was a riot," I said dryly.

"Oh, come on. Don't be like that," Cole said with a grin. "You know you were out of your element there. There's no shame in admitting that you're glad to be done with it."

But the bitch of it was that I wasn't. I wasn't glad. Sure, I was glad that Jessileigh was safe, but I still missed the kids. More than I ever thought I would. Me. The guy who pretty much never wanted to be anywhere near a person under the age of twenty-one, and I was missing a group of first graders. It was crazy!

"So I spoke to Mr. Vanderhall, and he said that you took care of having a case against his ex-wife. You were crucial to them being able to press charges and make sure that he got full custody of Jessileigh," Levi said, bringing things back to business.

I nodded. "I was able to identify her and the car. It wasn't a big deal."

"Hey," Levi said. "To them, it was a big deal. If you hadn't been there, that little girl would have been kidnapped or, even worse, badly hurt. You did good, Dec."

I didn't feel good. And again, not just physically. I knew that I had saved Jessileigh. I knew that I got her out of harm's way, but to what end? She was most likely never going to forget that moment—the moment her mother tried to run us over or when I essentially threw her out of the way. Thank God, Kristin had been standing right there, otherwise *I* could have been the one to hurt Jess.

Just the thought of that made my stomach clench.

I know that I made fun of this case from the beginning, I bitched about it from the get-go and said that it was a bullshit assignment, but the truth was, it had messed with my head almost as much as being back in Afghanistan.

"You okay?" Levi asked.

I shook my head. These guys were my best friends, my brothers, if I couldn't talk to them, I was screwed. "No. I'm not. I'm so fucking not."

"What's going on?" Sebastian asked.

Where did I even begin? "I got attached," I said. "I don't even know how or when or even why it happened, but I got attached to those kids. I never thought it was even possible and yet..."

"There's nothing wrong with that," Levi said. "That just shows that you're actually human. If you had been able to just walk away from all of them without any emotion, I'd have to question whether or not you actually have a heart." He took a pull from his beer. "Hell, I think that it's not that hard to get attached when you're on a case. I mean, it's happened to all of us."

"That's different," I said.

"How? How is it any different?" Levi asked.

"You fell in love with Harper," I snapped. "And you!" I

pointed at Sebastian. "You fell in love with Ali. It's completely different."

"And you fell in love with those kids," Levi said simply and then shrugged. "It's not a bad thing, Dec."

"That's not all he fell in love with," Cole muttered and leaned back in his chair.

I glared at him, hoping to intimidate him, but all he did was glare back.

"What? Am I fucking wrong? It's not just the kids, man. It's the kids, and Kristin and *her* kid. Just admit it."

"Don't we have business to discuss?" I asked, changing the subject. I'd already talked with Levi about all of this, and I wasn't looking to rehash it again. "What's the next case? Please tell me that it's something a little edgier than learning the words to Christmas songs." Levi and Sebastian exchanged glances, and I had an idea that something was up.

"Actually... that's something we need to discuss," Levi began. "We've had a lot of great clients, and the business is definitely growing. Honestly, I cannot even believe how many potential clients we have. I can realistically see us having to hire more guys by the end of the year."

"So that's a good thing, right?" Cole asked.

Levi nodded. "Definitely. The thing is, we've had some tame cases and some not-so-tame cases. We've each faced danger on at least one job, and while we can argue that it all goes with the territory, I for one feel like I have too much to lose to keep taking those kinds of risks."

Sebastian spoke up. "Levi and Harper are going to have

a baby. He's going to want to be based closer to home and not be traveling quite so much. Ali and I are getting married, and we want to have kids right away, and I know that I feel the same way. I'm not willing to be away from her for too long."

"So you're both a couple of pussies. How is that my problem?" Cole asked, sounding annoyed.

"Shut up," Levi snapped. "I'm thinking that maybe we cut back on the amount of... dangerous jobs we take."

"What difference will that make?" Cole chimed in again. "This job that Declan just finished was supposed to be a no-brainer, and he still got hurt. Shit can happen anywhere, at any time. You can't know in advance exactly what's going to happen."

"While that's true," Sebastian said, "I think we just need to be a little more... choosy... about the jobs that we take."

That all sounded fine and well to me. Maybe I'd actually get a say in future assignments and not draw the short straw and get something like Jess's case ever again. If anyone would have told me that protecting a six-year-old at school was going to get me banged up, I would have laughed in their face. Ha. The joke was obviously on me.

"Declan? What do you think?" Levi asked.

I shrugged. "Yeah. That's fine. Whatever."

Levi sighed. "Okay, fine. Don't have an opinion. That clears the way for us to talk about you and Kristin. To get everyone up to speed on what happened?"

I shrugged again, knowing that it was something that

was going to keep coming up until everyone knew it all. "She's scared. She lost her husband, her world got turned upside down. She doesn't want to go there again. Seeing me get hit by the car freaked her out. I know it wasn't easy, and she says that she doesn't want to put Lily through that, and I can respect that."

"So then this new solution with the business should work in your favor," Sebastian said. "You should be a little more excited about it."

"I don't know," I said miserably. "I don't know if it's too late. The damage may have already been done."

"Only one way to find out," Levi said right before he waved the waitress over to bring us another round of drinks.

I was a glutton for punishment.

I wonder if there was a group for that. Something like AA where you go and sit around with other people as twisted as you are. "Hello, my name is Declan Curtis, and I am a glutton for punishment."

Maybe I should start that group myself.

It was a Saturday, and I was supposed to be moving out of the extended-stay hotel and heading back to my place in DC, but where am I? Standing in a park behind a tree, watching Kristin push Lily on a swing. I was no better than a fucking stalker, and I didn't even care.

I was going to extend my stay at the hotel. I just

couldn't leave until I at least talked to Kristin and tried to see if she was open to giving me a chance. A second chance. Hell, a third, fourth or fifth fucking chance. I knew I was pushing my luck, but I didn't want to just walk away. This was supposed to just be a fling— I'm good at those. But this? This was so much more, and it scared the shit out of me, and yet it was even scarier to think of it totally being over.

How fucked-up is that?

I stepped out from behind the tree to get a better look at them, and Lily instantly spotted me.

"Mommy! Mommy! Look! It's Mr. Curtis, and he's still alive!"

I almost choked when I heard that, but before I knew it, Lily was hurling herself into my arms and hugging me. I dropped to my knees and held on for dear life. I'm not gonna lie, it hurt like hell—my ribs were still bruised—but it was worth the pain.

"Mr. Curtis! Are you all better now? Is your head okay? Do your ribs hurt? Are you coming back to school?" She was firing questions at me a million miles an hour, and it was the absolute greatest thing I'd heard in over a week.

I pulled back and looked down at her smiling face and felt my heart just kick. "Yes, I'm getting better. My head is fine, my ribs still hurt, but unfortunately, I won't be coming back to the school. I hear you've got a really great teacher now."

She nodded. "Mrs. O'Brien is really nice, and she

always starts the day with math. I got a one hundred and a star on my math test!"

"Good for you!"

She beamed up at me. "I got to have ice cream for dessert that night. Mommy said it was my reward."

"That's because she's the best, right?" Even as I said the words, I looked to where Kristin was standing—still too far away. I lifted Lily up and walked across the park, toward Kristin, and it didn't take long to see the wariness in her eyes. "Hey."

"Hi."

I put Lily down, and Kristin immediately pulled her close. As if she were trying to protect her from me. "How are you?"

"Fine," she said quietly.

"That's good," I said and smiled. It felt good just to look at her.

We were silent for a long time, and Kristin was the one to finally break it. "Um... we need to go. It's... it's getting late, and we have homework to do." She looked at me sadly. "Take care of yourself."

"Kristin, wait," I said, reaching out and placing my hand on her arm. "Can I... can I see you again?"

She didn't even think about it. She immediately shook her head no. "I'm sorry. We need to go."

And then they were gone.

Glutton for punishment. Take two.

Chuck called me and let me know that the kids had prepared a thank-you gift for me. I asked him if he could just mail it, but he said no. It was important for the kids to be able to say goodbye—especially after everything they'd heard about my saving Jessileigh.

So now here I was, walking into the school and being forced to be so close to Kristin and Lily and not being able to do a damn thing about it.

"Hi, Mr. Curtis," Rose said as I walked into the office.

I nodded and didn't get to say a word because Chuck walked out at that moment. "Come on, Declan. I'll walk down to the class with you. I know you're anxious to get in and out as quickly as possible."

That was both true and false, but I chose not to mention it. We walked silently down to the class, and Chuck knocked on the door before we walked in. Sandra O'Brien smiled at us and immediately called the kids to come and sit in a circle. She had a chair sitting at the top of the circle for me to sit in, and I almost turned and ran out.

"Okay, class. Let's all say hello to Mr. Curtis while you take your seats!"

Sure enough, the entire group sat in a perfect circle while calling out their greetings to me. Jessileigh was sitting on my right, and she reached up and grabbed my hand and squeezed it. Lily came and sat to my left and did the same thing.

I felt it all the way in my chest.

Once everyone was seated, Mrs. O'Brien came and

stood behind me and motioned for the kids to look at her. Then she held up her hand and counted to three. All at once, the entire class began to sing the song they had been learning for the Christmas pageant. They sounded so sweet and so wonderful that it brought tears to my eyes.

Or maybe I'm allergic to something. I'm not sure.

When they'd finished, I clapped hard and loud and told them how proud I was of all their hard work and how great they sounded.

"We made this for you," Jessileigh said as she stood and released my hand only to pick it up again a moment later when she handed me a giant card. "All of us drew a picture in it and signed our names."

Sure enough, the card stood about three feet tall, and it was brightly decorated with all kinds of pictures—animals, cars, Spiderman, rainbows—and underneath each work of art was the name of the artist. I almost felt like I couldn't breathe when I found Lily's name and saw that she drew a picture of the three of us—her, Kristin, and me. Like a family. I swallowed hard as I looked up at all their little expectant faces, my heart in my throat. "Thank you," I said quietly. "This is the best present I've ever gotten."

Fifteen minutes later, we left the room. I knew that the kids had music class to get to, and I didn't want to disrupt their day more than I already had. I walked with Chuck back down to the office and shook his hand.

"I want to thank you for all that you did while you were here, Declan. I know it was way out of your comfort zone, but you did a wonderful job with those kids. If you ever decide to change careers...," he said with a laugh.

I couldn't help but join in. It felt good. "Thanks, Chuck. But let's just say that I know my limitations." We shook hands again, and I watched as he walked into the office.

And Kristin walked out.

We stood there, frozen in place. "Hi," I said cautiously. This was so not the time or the place, and yet there was no way for me to just pretend that she wasn't right there.

"Hi." She looked around nervously and fidgeted with her hair and then looked down at the giant card in my hand. "You saw the kids." It was a statement, not a question.

I nodded. "They sang for me. It was great."

"Lily was really excited about it. They all wanted it to be perfect for you."

"It was amazing. They're going to be a big hit in the Christmas pageant," I said with a smile. "They're a great group of kids." The small talk was killing me. "Listen, can... can we step outside for a minute? Please?"

At first I thought she was going to just take off, but she took a deep breath as if to steady herself. "Declan, I can't do this. I can't... I thought that I could do the casual thing. And then I thought I could deal with getting involved with someone again. It turns out, I can't. I can't go through what I did with Nick again. Not even for you."

I took a step toward her and was relieved when she didn't take a step back. "Kristin, there are no guarantees in life. No one is guaranteed tomorrow. Are you really willing to go through life—missing out on living—because you're too afraid to take a risk?" I asked desperately. "What happened that day was a freak accident. Believe me, I didn't sign on for that either. I took Jess's case because it was supposed to be safe."

"But what about the next case? Or the one after that?" Tears began to form in her eyes, and they almost killed me. "I wouldn't survive it a second time. I can't do that to Lily."

"The guys and I talked. We're going to do less risky and dangerous cases. We're going to hire more guys. I... I'm trying here," I said, willing her to believe me.

She was silent for a long time. And then she wasn't. "I'm sorry," she whispered. "I'm really, really sorry." And then she turned and ran down the hall toward her class.

13

KRISTIN

SOMETIMES MAKING THE SMART DECISION HURTS LIKE HELL.

Sometimes making the smart decision feels like the worst thing you could have done.

This was definitely one of those times.

For more than a week now, I'd been telling and retelling myself that this was for the best, that both Lily and I would end up being devastated again if I chose to have a relationship with a man like Declan. And when he showed up at school, showing a side of himself that few even knew existed, it just twisted the knife in the pain.

But I was going to remain resolute. I wasn't going to cave, just because everything inside me was screaming to do so.

I was reminding myself yet again that this was for the best as Lily and I drove to the cemetery on Saturday morning where Nick was buried. It was a cold morning, and the car hadn't yet heated up, so my fingers were chilled and my cheeks felt chapped. My eyes ached from crying too much and not sleeping enough.

I glanced back and saw Lily was looking somber and reflective, bundled up in her red coat and hat and staring out the car window.

"What are you thinking about, sweetie?" I asked, worried that this was harder on her than it should have been. It was my fault. I should have been smarter from the beginning.

"I think Daddy would have liked his flowers," she said, meeting my eyes in the rearview mirror. She held in her lap a bundle of bright yellow daisies.

"Yes, I'm sure he would have."

"Can we go see him again on Christmas? And bring him Christmas flowers?"

My throat ached that she had to go through such a loss so young. "Of course we can. We can see him whenever you like."

"I would like to see him on Christmas morning," she said with a little nod. "After we open presents."

"After the presents it is."

This idea seemed to please her, and she turned to stare back out the window. It took fifteen minutes to reach the cemetery, and she didn't say anything else the whole time.

When we arrived, I took her hand as we walked toward Nick's grave.

Lily carefully laid the flowers next to the headstone. "These are for you, Daddy," she said. "I picked out yellow because it's a happy color and I hope you're happy. I bet heaven has a lot of yellow flowers."

My eyes burned as I thought about how much Nick had loved Lily and how little time he'd gotten to spend with her. The unfairness of it all hit me again and made me ache.

She turned suddenly to look at me over her shoulder. "Daddy wants us to be happy too, right?"

"Of course he does, baby. Of course he does."

The words settled on me strangely, although they weren't a new thought or a particularly profound one. But I felt them in my chest as Lily turned back to face Nick's headstone.

Lily began to talk to her father again, as she always did, filling him in on various things that had happened since our last visit. She talked about Mrs. O'Brien and how well she'd been doing in math. She talked about Jessileigh and how much nicer she was than she'd originally thought.

Then she told him about Mr. Curtis and how, at first, she didn't think he was a good teacher, but he was better than she'd thought. And how he'd saved Jessileigh. And how he liked Mommy. And how he had the nicest laugh that made other people laugh too. And that he was the best Mad Hatter to have at a tea party.

My eyes burned again as I listened, but I didn't try to stop her. It wouldn't be right to keep her from working through the things in her life, especially something that had had such a big impact.

"Mommy says we won't see him anymore, and she's sad about it, but she pretends not to be."

"Lily—" I broke off the automatic comment since I had no idea what to say.

Lily had paused for me to continue, but when I didn't, she focused again on her father. "I miss him now too. I miss both you and him."

So my throat was aching again now, and it kept aching as Lily finished her conversation with her father and took my hand to show she was ready to leave.

I kissed my fingertips and leaned down to press them onto the cold gravestone, desperately wishing that, for once, life could be easy and simple.

It just never was.

We walked back to the car in silence, and I hugged and kissed Lily before she got into her seat.

When I started the car and put it into drive, Lily said in that seemingly random way she had, "I'm glad we knew Daddy. Even if we didn't have him very long."

For just a moment my vision darkened, and when it returned, it was with the kind of blinding revelation that sometimes hits you out of the blue.

She was right. My ever-intuitive six-year old was right.

Having Nick was worth it—for however short a time we were given him. I wouldn't trade that time we had together for anything in the world. None of us are guaranteed forever, let alone tomorrow. We need to make the most of the time that we have right now.

By the time we'd reached the house again, I knew exactly what we needed to do.

On Monday afternoon, I was so anxious and exhilarated, at the same time, I could barely focus on the last class block. I'd planned everything out to the last detail, but I couldn't be absolutely sure of the outcome.

I'd hurt Declan. I knew that. And he might have decided his interest in me just wasn't worth the trouble.

I had a lot of baggage that would always complicate a relationship.

But I knew I needed to try, so I sat in Chuck's office after school had ended, trying to breathe slowly and not get too worked up about what was about to happen.

After several minutes of waiting, I heard voices outside of the mostly closed office door.

"This is ridiculous, Chuck," Declan said with just a hint of annoyance. "I'm not a teacher anymore. I can't be summoned to a meeting like this."

"I know, and I appreciate you coming. One of the parents from your class was very insistent that she meet with you. She wouldn't stop nagging until I made an appointment, and I, of course, wasn't about to give out your personal information to her. This seemed like the best option."

"Okay, but if she just called me in to yell at me, then I'm out of here."

"I'm sure she's prepared to be reasonable. Just listen to what she says."

I almost smiled at how well Chuck was handling it. I'd had to ask him to do this for me as a favor, but he'd been very willing—evidently realizing the real situation and thinking it was rather amusing.

I didn't think it was amusing. Or not much. I mostly just wanted it over with.

Maybe Declan would say he didn't want to see me again after everything that had happened, everything I had put him through, but I had to at least try.

The office door opened then, and Declan was standing in the doorway. He looked as handsome as ever but too tired.

My heart gave a little skip at the sight of him.

He jerked to a halt and stood frozen as he processed my presence. His eyes looked slightly dazed as he stared, as if he couldn't quite believe it was me.

I stood up. "Hi," I said rather stupidly.

He opened his mouth and then shut it again.

I glanced over his shoulder at Chuck. "Thanks, Chuck," I said with a little smile.

He winked and closed the office door behind Declan.

"You're the parent," Declan said at last.

"I'm the parent."

"And you're not here to yell at me about being a crap teacher." Realization was starting to wash over his face, and something started to smolder in its place.

"You weren't a crap teacher."

He gave me a significant look.

"Okay, you weren't the best teacher ever, but you did okay. And I'm not here to yell at you."

"Then why are you here?" He stepped forward and started to reach out toward me before he stopped himself.

I reached out and took his hand instead. "I'm here because I changed my mind."

"You changed..."

"...my mind."

He froze for just a moment. "About..."

"About us. Everything."

His tight expression suddenly relaxed, and I let out my pent breath with a *whoosh* since I could see the answer on his face, in the wash of something akin to joy.

"If you still want me," I added when he didn't say anything.

He made a choked sound and took my face in both his hands. "Of course I still want you. I'll always want you. I've been miserable. I thought it was your final answer and I'd have to spend my life without you." His eyes scanned my face. "I didn't want to spend my life without you. Without Lily."

I couldn't seem to stop smiling. "I thought it was my final answer too, but I was wrong. It was wrong not to take what was offered, just because I was afraid of losing it. I will have a lot to work through. I mean, with your job, I'm going to be... to be overly anxious for a while. But I promise I'll work on it. I want you as you are, and I'm not going to cut Lily and me off from something so good, just because there's risk involved. A wise man once told me there's risk in everything. There's risk in life. But there are such good things too, and I want to have as much of the good things in life that I can. I want it for Lily and me. And for you."

I felt kind of stupid after the rambling, earnest speech, but from the expression on Declan's face, he evidently appreciated it. "I want it for all of us too," he said. "And I am going to be careful about the kinds of jobs I take. Taking risks just isn't as easy as it used to, not if I have so much to lose."

We were both smiling like idiots as he leaned down to kiss me. And the kiss was eager and happy and a little sloppy, but neither of us seemed to care.

When he pulled back, I reached out to hug him, and he wrapped his strong arms around me, holding me so tightly I couldn't breathe for a moment.

It felt about right to me.

As close to perfect as we could get.

We talked for a little while and I realized we'd better give Chuck back his office. When we got up to leave, I texted Nick's parents so they could bring Lily back to the school. It wasn't easy explaining to them that I'd met someone. That I was ready to have a future with someone. Luckily, they understood. They wanted me to be happy. Knew that Nick would want me to be happy.

They'd taken her out for donuts with the understanding that, if things went bad with Declan, she'd spend the afternoon with them. But otherwise they'd bring her back to the school.

So Declan and I were standing on the sidewalk as the van pulled up and Lily jumped out, almost before it had come to a complete stop.

She hurled herself at Declan, and he scooped her up in a hug, laughing.

"Are you back?" she asked, her voice muffled by his shirt. "For good this time?"

He was grinning as he put her back on her feet, and I was grinning too. "Yes, I'm back." And then he looked at me. "For good."

"Oh, good. Me and Mommy missed you a lot."

I could see by the look on Declan's face that that little admission meant the world to him.

"Mommy and I," I corrected automatically.

"See?" Lily said, beaming. "Mommy and I missed you a lot."

Declan attended the school Christmas pageant.

He was right there in the front row as each of the classes did their thing, and his first grade class sang their song just to him. They were a bit off-key and distracted, and one of the boys pulled the hair of one of the girls and made her cry on stage, but Declan gave them a standing ovation just the same.

It was hard to believe it was the same man, but I knew it was just the real man coming out at last. Declan was at heart a family man who had never had a family.

Until now.

We took Lily out for cupcakes after the pageant, and then he came home with us. Once Lily went to bed that evening, we spent the night together. It was the happiest evening I could remember—the kind I didn't think I'd be able to have again after Nick died.

And the best thing was I could foresee so many more happy days and nights in the future.

On Christmas morning, I woke up with that heavy feeling of joy and anticipation in my gut.

It felt kind of like when I was a kid, when the day was filled with excitements and pleasures untold.

The first thing I saw was Declan, one arm flung up above his head and the covers pushed down to his chest.

I smiled at the sight.

I was still smiling when he mumbled something and blinked a few times, turning his head toward me. "You woke me up," he said.

"I didn't say a thing."

"Your staring woke me up."

"Well, I can't do anything about that. You're just so adorable when you're sleeping that I couldn't help myself."

This comment was rewarded with him rolling on top of me. I giggled and kissed him back. "Merry Christmas," I murmured against his lips.

"Merry Christmas to you too. I can't remember the last time I was so excited about Christmas. I can't wait for you and Lily to open your presents."

I could tell he meant it. Even having just awakened, his eyes were full of affection and good spirits. It filled me with a kind of awed happiness that a man like Declan was so invested in Lily and me.

"You can give me my present now if you want a head start," I told him brightly.

He chuckled. "Nice try."

"You could just tell me what it is, and then I'd still act surprised."

"Not a chance."

"You're kind of mean."

"And you're kind of pushy."

"I guess we deserve each other then."

"I don't know if I deserve you," he said, his expression shifting slightly, "but I'm sure as hell glad that I have you."

We kissed again—soft and leisurely—until we heard the sound of feet running in the hallway. Declan groaned and rolled off me as Lily called out at the top of her lungs, "I'm awake! I'm awake! It's Christmas!"

"We'll be out in a minute," I called back.

I giggled at Declan's face. "One of the joys of having a kid."

His face softened into a smile. "I wouldn't miss it for the world."

I was filled with so much feeling and affection that I couldn't possibly contain it.

"What?" he asked, sitting up and giving me a curious look.

I shook my head.

"What?" he demanded again.

"Nothing. Just that I love you."

I really couldn't believe I'd actually said it out loud. Surely it was too soon. I didn't want to spook him or make him feel trapped.

His expression as he processed the words looked anything but trapped. His face broke into joy. "Good. Because I sure as hell love you too. And it's going to be for forever."

"Hurry up!" Lily yelled from outside the door. "It's time for presents!"

We were both laughing as we got up and put on some more clothes. Then we went out to find Lily and make coffee and waffles before we opened Christmas presents.

As she was looking at the Christmas tree with her mouth full of food, Lily burst out, "Merry Christmas to us!"

Declan and I couldn't help but agree.

EPILOGUE
DECLAN

"Here's to the new year," I said as I held up my beer. Levi, Sebastian, and Cole did the same, and we all saluted.

Actually, the New Year had started a little over a week ago, but this was the first time the four of us were together—and alone. New Year's Eve had been great. Levi and Harper were there. I still couldn't believe they were having a baby. Even looking at Levi now, the sappy grin hadn't left his face.

Seb and Ali were there—decked out like they were going to the Academy Awards or something. Sebastian's family had made them put in an appearance at the annual Maxwell New Year's Ball. I was thankful that the rest of us hadn't gotten sucked into that one.

Looking over at Cole, I frowned. He was a damn mystery. Oh, he had been at the New Year's party— Hell, he'd even brought a date. But he wasn't happy. He wasn't relaxed. After all this time he still wasn't comfortable in his own skin, and it was starting to worry me.

"As much as I loved seeing everyone and celebrating last week," Levi said, "this is still better." He motioned to the four of us just sitting around a table in our favorite pub.

"Here, here," Seb said and took a pull of his drink.

"Yeah, yeah, yeah... great to be here. What's next on the schedule?" Cole asked, seemingly agitated.

Levi sent him a pointed glare before clearing his throat. "Our schedule is relatively clear for the month of January. I did that intentionally so that we can train the two new guys. I want them to spend a week with each of us. I think we all bring something unique to the table, and I want them to feel comfortable when we put them on their first cases come February."

"I'm not holding anyone's fucking hand," Cole snapped.

A loud collective sigh came from around the table. "No one said hand holdings," Levi said. "I just want those guys to know what they're doing and to understand the kind of work that we do."

"Whatever."

"So what does that mean for the rest of us come February?" I asked.

"We're going to start looking at computer security and doing consultations for the private sector. I think it's the best of both worlds. We still get to do what we love, without putting ourselves in the line of fire. And I know I can't speak for all of us, but I'm looking forward to spending time closer to home." And there was that sappy grin again.

"How's Harper feeling?" Seb asked.

"She's good. A little morning sickness, but other than that, she's feeling really good. Her parents are over the moon about the baby."

"Have you started planning anything yet?" I asked. "Names? Nursery?" As soon as the words were out of my mouth, I wanted to groan. A couple of months ago, I couldn't have cared less about kids, families, nursery's... but now? I thought about Lily's room and how Kristin had painted the mural on the wall and how they spent time every night before bed, reading stories. A smile crossed my face. The thought of experiencing that someday with a child of my own wasn't nearly as unappealing or scary as it once was.

"Wipe that fucking grin off your face," Cole growled. "I expected that with Levi and even Seb, but you? You were supposed to be on my side and leave all that marriage and baby crap to them."

I shrugged and took a drink. "Believe me, I'm just as shocked as you are. It completely snuck up on me, but I don't regret it for a minute."

Cole snorted with disgust.

"The only thing we've decided is that if it's a boy, we're going to name him Gavin."

We all fell silent.

It doesn't seem to matter how much time passes, just

the mention of Gavin's name and I felt like I'd been kicked in the gut. My heart was racing, and I could feel myself beginning to sweat. Everything about that day, that hour, that minute comes rushing back to me. Why was it that I was here and he was not?

Survivor's guilt. Yeah, I got it. Everyone kept telling me that it was normal, but would they still be saying that if they knew that it was my fault—that it was my distraction—that cost my friend his life?

I hated it. Hated this. The fact that the four of us were sitting here and talking calmly about our futures and how we were hiring other guys to take on the more dangerous cases so that we could all sit back and be safe. Gavin didn't have that option.

"My in-laws were a little shocked that we wanted to do it," Levi said, interrupting my thoughts, "but we told them that it was the best way to honor Gavin."

"I think that's awesome," Sebastian said. "Gavin would've liked that."

And the thing was, he would have, I thought. Gavin loved his sister so damn much and was so proud of everything that she did, and there wasn't a doubt in my mind that if he had lived and was here now, he would be doting on her and making sure Levi was taking care of her.

Which he was.

I sat back and listened to him talk a little more about how he felt about becoming a father, and it had me thinking about Lily. And Kristin.

There was no way that I could ever replace Nick. Not for either of them. But it was an intimidating position to be in. I want to be Kristin's husband. I want to be Lily's father. But Nick was always going to be there. And I knew that it wasn't fair to him. I knew that I was going to love and take care of them both, but—especially in Lily's case—I had to be careful to not overstep and make her feel like I'm trying to replace her father.

If she wanted to call me Declan for the rest of my life, I'd be fine with it. But if she ever wants to call me dad... well... just the thought of it was like someone squeezing my heart.

So there we sat. Levi was just starting his family. I'd stepped into a ready-made one. Sebastian and Ali would be getting married soon, and I knew that they'll be in the same position before too long.

And then there was Cole.

He was clearly distracted as Levi talked, and I couldn't blame him. Before Kristin and Lily, I probably would have been scanning the room, looking for something else to do while Levi talked about the joys of pregnancy and decorating nurseries.

But it was something more.

He was angry about the turn of events within our company. He'd been vocal since day one about our taking on less dangerous cases. It was like he had a death wish. Hell, I think we all did when we first came home. We didn't feel worthy of being alive, being able to walk around each day and be around our friends and families. We each did things that we didn't want to do because we didn't think we deserved to be happy.

Levi went to work with his father—which he swore he'd never do.

Sebastian went to work with his father—which he despised.

And me? Hell, I just wandered around and refused to settle anywhere because it's harder to hit a moving target. I was happy moving from place to place and keeping everything superficial because I didn't want to make connections. Didn't want to care about anyone.

Because it hurt too much when you lost them.

And then I met Kristin.

She made me want to stay in one place. Made me want to stay grounded and put down roots. And it felt really good to actually feel alive again.

Cole needed that. He needs to find that place—where he was comfortable with himself, comfortable in his skin and where he could live in the present and look forward to the future rather than staying in the past.

I know he had a lot of baggage—shitty upbringing, abusive parents, time in a gang—he'd been there, done that, and yet he didn't see how far he'd come. In his own mind, he was still that punk.

He'd keep taking the shitty cases that no one wants because they're too dangerous. Hell, he'd probably even search them out himself. Eventually the guys and I would have to do something drastic to make him stop running.

That was what Levi and Seb did for me. They saw something in me that told them I needed to stop running.

Who knew it would take a classroom full of six-year-olds to make that happen?

And you know what? I don't regret it for a minute. I know I was a prick in the beginning and I went into the case kicking and screaming and bitching. Hell, what did I know? Turned out that my friends really did look out for me and maybe, just maybe, knew what was best for me.

I looked over at Cole again. Levi was done talking babies, so Cole was back in the conversation. We'd let him be for now. I had to make a mental note to talk to Levi and Seb about cases that I thought would benefit Cole. When the time was right. Right now? We all had enough on our plates. There were new guys to train and lives to settle into.

And for the first time in a long time, I was actually looking forward to the future.

ABOUT SAMANTHA CHASE

New York Times and USA Today Bestseller/contemporary romance writer Samantha Chase released her debut novel, Jordan's Return, in November 2011. Although she waited until she was in her 40's to publish for the first time, writing has been a lifelong passion. Her motivation to take that step was her students: teaching creative writing to elementary age students all the way up through high school and encouraging those students to follow their writing dreams gave Samantha the confidence to take that step as well.

When she's not working on a new story, she spends her time reading contemporary romances, blogging, playing way too many games of Scrabble on Facebook and spending time with her husband of 25 years and their two sons in North Carolina. For more information visit her website at www.chasing-romance.com.

Sign up for her mailing list and get exclusive content and chances to win members-only prizes!

http://bit.ly/1jqdxPR

ABOUT NOELLE ADAMS

Noelle handwrote her first romance novel in a spiral-bound notebook when she was twelve, and she hasn't stopped writing since. She has lived in eight different states and currently resides in Virginia, where she writes full time, reads any book she can get her hands on, and offers tribute to a very spoiled cocker spaniel.

She loves travel, art, history, and ice cream. After spending far too many years of her life in graduate school, she has decided to reorient her priorities and focus on writing contemporary romances. For more information, please check out her website: noelle-adams.com.

If you want to keep up with her new releases and sales, you can sign up for her monthly newsletter.

If you want book discussion and insider information on her books, you can join her Reader Group on Facebook. Just ask to join and she'll approve you.

About Noelle Adams

If you want a complete list of her books, including series and tropes, you can go to her Printable Book List.

Made in United States
Orlando, FL
05 July 2022